Child Out of Place

A Story of New England

By
Patricia Q. Wall

Illustrations by Debby Ronnquist

FALL ROSE BOOKS
Kittery Point, Maine
www.fallrosebooks.com

This is a work of fiction. Names, characters, places and incidents are either the product of the author's imagination or, if real, are used fictitiously.

CHILD OUT OF PLACE: A Story of New England
© Copyright 2004 Patricia Q. Wall

Illustrations © Copyright 2004 by Debby Ronnquist

Third Printing

Published by
FALL ROSE BOOKS
P.O.Box 39
Kittery Point, Maine 03905
www.fallrosebooks.com

ISBN: 0-9742185-0-2
Library of Congress control number: 2003108267
    1.Slavery - Juvenile Fiction
    2.Slavery - New England - History - Juvenile Fiction
    3.Afro-American - History - Juvenile Fiction
    4.Afro-American - History - Portsmouth (NH) - Juvenile Fiction
Design by ad-cetera graphics
Printed in the United States of America

To my children, Bradford, Lawrence and Valerie.
Your loving encouragement kept me going, kept me
believing that Matty's story could and needed to be told.

Imagination can never fill in for history's neglect. Yet, for the sake of even a glimmer of understanding, we must try. From recorded stray bits, chance mentions, and those disheartening lists of one-name and no-name enslaved Africans this imagined story came forth.

Prologue
BOSTON, MASSACHUSETTS
23 December 1863

My name is Matty — Matty Warren Smith Johnson. This morning I have decided, especially on this particular date in December, that I should finally take pen in hand to write down a story about my family. (Besides, I need the distraction. I've got to get my mind off worrying about my brave soldier grandsons, the two of them, fighting in that awful war down south.)

I am seated by the front window of my third floor bedroom — me and my scraggly old cat, Marble. From our vantage point here, back of Beacon Hill, he and I usually spend our time watching the comings and goings on the busy street below. But today, I'll leave the watching to the cat. In my mind I am journeying north of Boston to another seaport town and a house where my story takes place.

I will always remember the old Warren mansion in

Portsmouth, New Hampshire, with mixed emotions. It is where I was born and where my family toiled for almost three quarters of a century in slavery. I cannot bring my adult self to think of that place as home for I did not belong there. None of us did. And yet, a part of me, the child I once was, sometimes reaches back to it with longing.

If I were to allow my tired, elderly feet to walk Portsmouth's streets today and stand before the Warren mansion on Daniel Street, I would see just an elegant brick building, gracefully aging behind tall elm trees. The commercial and waterfront neighborhood crowding in upon it also aging, though far less gracefully.

Perhaps, I would follow the stepping-stone sidewalk around the mansion's west corner to view a small, attached wooden structure at the back — the slaves' house. Then, I would let my eyes travel up its clapboarded side to a tiny second floor window of the room where I was born. Of course I would not linger there for long or knock on any door. Instead, I would turn my back, cross the quiet dirt street, and go in search of friends who might still be living in the town.

But that child part of me, she would long to stay behind, at least for a while. That tall, skinny youngster that I was back in 1806, she would likely settle herself down on the front steps of Mr. Warren's general merchandise store. Then, she would happily stare across Daniel Street at the front door of the mansion she once loved. She would delight in seeing the handsome, three-story building again, its many tall windows and, best of all, on the rooftop, a small round, six-windowed cupola — her special place, her 'glory' place, she called it.

Young Matty would also see a far different Portsmouth than I would. In her time it was a busy, prosperous seaport town. Its many wharves jutting out into the Piscataqua River were crowded, bowsprit to stern, with coastal and ocean-going sailing ships. And Daniel Street, one of the main arteries between waterfront and town center at Market Square, was often filled with exciting daytime traffic — on foot and on horseback.

But, reality would soon return to my adult's mind and I would recall that my youthful, innocent view of Portsmouth and that mansion did not last. By late December of 1806, I was forced to learn of the real world around me, one disdainful and sometimes hostile to my race. It was then that I began to feel like a child out of place, a child with little hope for a happy future.

Chapter One
PORTSMOUTH, NEW HAMPSHIRE
23 December 1806

*S*wirling snow enveloped the small rooftop cupola of the Warren mansion that afternoon. Sleet battered its narrow windows. Matty found it nearly impossible to see even the snow-clogged streets far below.

"I won't find any glory out there," she grumbled. "Nothing but snow...boring snow."

The not-quite-ten-year-old girl started to turn away from the window, then she changed her mind. Blowing her breath against a cold windowpane, she began drawing a face. Her fingertip squeaked as she made a circle and topped it with short, tight curls. Next came large eyes, a broad nose and then, she paused. In one quick stroke, she drew a mouth turned down. Tears welled up as she recognized her face, her mood.

"I mustn't cry anymore...just mustn't. I got to be brave, like Papa said."

Misery as well as cold settled in around her as she

slumped down on part of a wooden bench which encircled the interior of the tiny six windowed tower. Now and then, gusty winds rattled old windowpanes, sending icy drafts swirling around her. But Matty was not about to be driven from the room. She pulled her muslin dust cap down over her ears and drew a knitted brown shawl tighter across her thin shoulders. With bare legs tucked up under two long woolen petticoats and a gray cotton dress, this child servant and former slave held to her perch.

"I'm not leaving. It's my time for being up here. They won't be needing me 'til suppertime."

Matty reached down into a large sewing basket, fished around among a pile of mending and pulled out a man's white silk stocking. It had a small hole in the toe and a worn place on the heel. Sighing to herself, she inserted a wooden darning egg and set about weaving a patch with needle and thread. In her head she could hear her grandmother Bess's stern and often repeated instructions.

"I expect neat stitches, girl, and no lumpiness. And mind you keep busy while you're up in that cupola, staring about and daydreaming."

Most afternoons, once Matty had finished serving the midday meal to her former master, the elderly Joshua Warren and his wife Caroline, she was permitted to visit the cupola. Eager for sights of a busy city, the youngster would scamper up to the third floor and then climb steep, narrow, winding steps up into the tower, her 'glory place'.

Disappointed today at not being able to see any interesting distractions outside, Matty began to console herself with daydreams.

"Gotta get my head going on happier thoughts," she whispered. "I can't keep worrying about Papa and... everything."

She began by recalling other days in the cupola, days when that tiny room was warm and comforting, surrounded by bright glorious sunshine. Then, as she always loved to do, she imagined herself dressed as a beautiful queen with a crown of flowers, gazing down on her kingdom — the crowded seaport town of Portsmouth.

She smiled as she populated a snow-free Daniel Street, out front, with horse-drawn wagons, elegant carriages and horseback riders. Some she sent galloping up to Market Square at the center of town. Others were hurried down to the Piscataqua River, a block east of the mansion, where sailing ships and their exciting cargo waited.

In her imagination, Matty added the drumbeat sounds she always heard as vehicles and riders pounded along the hard-packed dirt streets. Each time they came to a street intersection, horseshoes and iron wheel rims clattered and screeched across pairs of wide steppingstone crosswalks. Matty enjoyed that racket, especially on busy market days.

To the scene, she added small herds of sheep, pigs, and cattle which occasionally clogged Daniel Street as farmers urged them on toward ships destined for Boston or farther south. She wrinkled her nose, thinking of all the horse and other animal manure that constantly littered the roads before being ground down by passing traffic.

Matty then gave her thoughts to the human foot traffic, that part of the daily scene she loved most. Depending on the season of the year and the day of the week, there would be various tradesmen heading for Market Square or simply selling their goods door to door. Fishmongers carried wooden trays of shimmering cod or black, slippery eels. Farmers pushed carts loaded with fresh vegetables, tubs of pale white butter, cheeses and brown eggs, nestled in straw.

Her favorite tradesman was the Water Street baker's son. In his tattered, tri-corner hat and patched blue jacket, the handsome boy would swagger past the mansion, a great basket of fresh bread on each arm. Sometimes, Matty could see small, golden sugar cakes tucked to one side of the crusty round loaves.

Along the stone-paved sidewalks of Daniel Street, well-dressed business men went about on their important matters. Women in pretty dresses and bonnets came by, sometimes with a child or two clinging to their long skirts. Their destination was usually Mr. Warren's general merchandise store directly across the street from the mansion's front door. And, wherever Matty looked, the faces which she saw — with rarely an exception — were white.

Until two weeks ago, this young girl had looked upon such scenes with wide-eyed enjoyment and hopefulness. That will be my life someday, she kept telling herself. When my papa comes back for me, I shall have pretty clothes and money for shopping. And, I'll live just as good as those white folks do.

For nearly five years, despite her father, Peter's, continuing and unexplained absence, Matty doggedly clung to her dreams.

"I won't be gone long," he called to her that morning in May of 1802 as the ship carrying him eased out into the swift, boiling current of the Piscataqua River. "I'll try to come back for you by Christmas." But that holiday came and went without his return.

"Never you mind, little one," Bess consoled her tearful granddaughter, "your papa will most likely be back before another Christmas comes around. You just keep up your courage."

And so Matty had. She held onto her belief that the next Christmas or surely the one after that, would be the time when her father would magically reappear.

However, in this winter of 1806, her belief was slipping badly. And, the passage of time was only part of the reason. One evening, in the middle of this December, her grandmother had begun telling Matty the sad, dreadful truth about her family's history and of their long enslavement in Portsmouth.

"I don't care what Gramma Bess says," Matty's angry voice now suddenly bounced off the cupola windows, "I won't stop hoping."

Smudging away fresh tears with her fist, the girl tried again to look outside. If only I could see down to the river and the wharf where Papa sailed away, she thought, I might feel a little closer to him.

But heavy falling snow continued to block her view. Matty settled back down to her sewing while her creative mind searched about for some other comforting daydream to pass the time. And, before long, one came forth, one she always enjoyed.

⸺ ❖ ⸺

Tuesday, 5 May 1802

"Matty, you just stay put until we're all ready to go," Bess called out, "and stop your fidgeting. Your new dress will be a mess of wrinkles."

"Yes, Gramma." Five year-old Matty hated sitting still. She was perched in the middle of a large, high back wooden settle. That ancient worn bench usually faced the fireplace but on this occasion it was turned around to face the open room. Restlessly, the child swung her short legs while inspecting her family's "everything" room. That's what her Uncle Ned called the first floor of their small two-story house. Connected to a back corner of the Warren mansion, that wood structure had been put in place as a slaves' house almost ninety years before.

It looks so different in here, little Matty thought, all cleared away and fixed up. And I smell fresh gingerbread, but I don't see it anywhere. Gramma must be hiding it.

Their "everything" room did have an expectant atmosphere that warm spring afternoon. Off to one side, under an open window, was a long pine table covered with a neat gingham cloth. A bowl of buttercups and blue forget-me-nots decorated the center.

Usually that table stood in the middle of the room, cluttered at one end with an assortment of Ned's tools, shoe repair projects and such. The other end was used for food preparation and sit-down meals.

"Gramma, where are Uncle Ned's tools and...and why are all our chairs scattered around the room?"

"Because we've got company coming this evening. You know that."

Impatiently, Bess smoothed out some wrinkles in the skirt of her best black dress. She and her twin brother, Ned, were standing near the front door which connected with the mansion.

"Why are we having company?" Matty persisted.

"Hush your questions, child." Bess turned to help her brother with his jacket. She brushed off bits of lint and then straightened the back of his collar.

Only in their faces did this sixty-year-old pair resemble one another. All else was different. Bess stood shorter than Ned by several inches and her stout body, covered in long skirts, made her look like a nicely rounded pear. Despite her weight, Bess always carried herself with a quiet dignity and a back nearly ram-rod straight. Her wide-set, dark brown eyes behind small spectacles looked upon the world with a no-nonsense attitude.

In contrast, her brother's six-foot, skinny frame had become slightly bent over with age, though his walk was still spry. Instead of Bess's curly gray hair beneath a dust cap, Ned's hatless head was nearly bald, his face clean shaven except for sideburns. His dark brown eyes beneath bushy, gray brows revealed a gentle, thoughtful man, but one with a keen sense of humor. He and Matty were great pals.

A quick stomping of boots from the floor above sent Matty's eyes toward a partially enclosed stairway to the left of the front door. Forgetting her grandmother's instructions, the child slipped off the bench and ran to greet her tall, young father as he bounded down the steps two at a time.

"There's my girl," said Peter, sweeping Matty up high before setting her down again. "You look pretty as a new penny."

"Gramma says we're having company," she chirped.

"Of course we are," laughed Peter. "This is our big day. We're going to celebrate."

"What's cela...cela...what's that?" asked Matty.

"Now Peter, don't get the child started on her endless questions," said Bess. "We've got to go now. We mustn't keep Mr. Warren waiting."

Peter winked at his daughter and whispered, "We're going to celebrate our freedom day."

Before Matty could ask about that, Bess leaned down and turned Matty to face her. "Child, you listen, now. When we go up town with Mr. Warren you are to be on your best behavior. Mind you keep silent. Let the grownups do the talking. If you've got questions, you just keep them in your head until we get back home. Understand?"

"Yes, Gramma." Matty shrank back from her grand-mother's stern look. Must be something scary we got to do, she thought.

"Bess, no need to get yourself all fussed and worried," said Ned. "Everything's going to be just fine."

"Of course it is," said Peter, kissing his mother's cheek. "Our freedom papers are waiting in the town clerk's office right now. All we got to do is go sign them."

"Well, I won't feel easy until we get them safe in our hands." Saying that, Bess turned and led the way out of their house and into the mansion.

Their route took the family into an attached entryway which also served as a pantry, then a left turn into the large kitchen of the mansion. Not stopping, they proceeded on into a broad hallway leading to the front of the mansion.

"Good afternoon, everyone," said Joshua Warren, standing by the open front door.

"Good afternoon, Sir." Bess, Ned and Peter replied almost in unison.

"Good 'noon, Sir," Matty piped up, then quickly covered her mouth as she glanced up at her grandmother.

Joshua Warren merely smiled, then settled his old fashioned cocked hat on his stringy gray hair and turned his attention to getting safely down the stone front steps. Except for his white stockings and shirt, he was dressed in black: coat, waistcoat, breeches and shoes. With the aid of a gold-headed cane, the eighty-one-year-old gentleman cleared the steps and set off at a surprisingly brisk pace up Daniel Street toward Market Square. If he had any thoughts about this occasion or about the family of his soon-to-be-freed slaves who followed him, he said nothing at all.

By the time everyone had silently walked the two blocks to the Square, past houses, a busy tavern and shops, little Matty's head was chock full of questions she wasn't allowed to ask. And, once they had climbed to the second floor of the Market House and presented themselves before the town clerk, the child's curiosity was too much to bear.

"Papa, what are we doing here? Who's that man?" Fearfully, Matty, looked up into the cold, staring, bespectacled eyes of the clerk seated at his cluttered desk.

"Hush child. Not now," whispered Peter.

"I want to go home," Matty whimpered. But one look at her grandmother's frowning face silenced further protest.

In the stuffy, book-lined office, the process of freeing

the African family proceeded with little comment. Off to one side of the room, two clerk's assistants seated at their high, slanted desks, never even looked up from their writing. At times, the soft scratching of their quill pens was the only noise to be heard.

Mr. Warren stepped forth to sign several documents on the clerk's desk and then he seated himself in a chair beside the desk. In turn, Bess, Ned and Peter each came forward to sign their document. From outside in the Square, a steeple bell tolled the hour of five o'clock.

"It's your turn, Matty," said her father, lifting her up to lean over the desk. "I'll hold the pen and guide your mark."

The feathery tip of the white quill tickled Matty's nose as she watched her hand being made to form a careful, neat 'X' at the bottom of a brief document. Setting his daughter down again, Peter and the others waited while the clerk added his signature to each document. Then Peter politely thanked Mr. Warren and the clerk, but Bess and Ned said nothing. Showing no emotion, the elderly twins simply picked up their documents and stood to one side while their now former master left the room ahead of them.

To Matty's great disappointment, as the family headed home, her flood of new questions either fell on deaf ears or received only short, unsatisfactory answers.

Later on, back in their house, Peter sat down on the bench and drew Matty onto his lap. Ned had gone into the mansion's kitchen to stoke up the fire in preparation for cooking the Warrens' supper. Bess was about to go upstairs to change into her work clothes when she heard her son talking to Matty. She stopped at the bottom of the steps to listen.

"Child, this paper is your freedom document," Peter said, " and you must never, ever lose it. It says you are not a slave anymore. See, it has your name on it." Matty hadn't any idea what "slave" meant, but her small fingers reached out to touch where her father was pointing.

"This is your first name," he said, "the one we gave you. That second word spells Warren. Of course that's not our family's true name."

"What is our true name, Papa?"

"No one knows," he replied. "It's been lost. But don't you worry your head about that. I intend to find a right name for our family soon."

"Peter," Bess called out, "that's foolishness. That document is meant to protect us under the law. We could be in danger if you put any other name on it."

Peter ignored his mother. "Matty, this document means we are free to leave here. We can go live wherever we want to."

"But Papa," asked a bewildered Matty, "why would we leave here? Isn't this our home?"

"No!" came his angry reply. "This isn't our home. We don't belong here, child. We never did. We're only here because slavers forced your great grandparents to come here a long time ago."

"Oh, Peter, stop!" called Bess. "You're frightening her. She's too young for all that now."

"Well, she's got to learn about it sometime," he replied.

"And she will, but not now." Bess headed on up the stairs. "You just talk to her about something else. And keep her out of mischief until Ned and I get back from the mansion."

By now, Matty was feeling so overwhelmed by all she had seen and heard, she couldn't think what question to ask next. Instead, she curled herself tighter against her father's chest and closed her eyes.

"Matty," Peter spoke quietly, "there is something else I need to talk to you about. And...and I don't want you to get upset. Understand?" The child merely nodded her head without looking up.

"In a few days," he said, " I'll be going away on a ship. Now it will only be for a short time." He hurried on, hoping to keep Matty calm. "Then I'll come right back for you. Your gramma and Uncle Ned have decided to stay here and keep on working for Mr. Warren, but I want to find a good paying job and a special place for us to live, one that's safe... a place where we will really belong."

"When will you come back?" asked a sleepy Matty.

"I'm not sure, Little One, but I'll be back as soon as I can. You just be my brave girl."

"Matty? Hey up there, Matty." Ned's deep voice rumbled up from the bottom of the cupola steps, disrupting the girl's daydreaming. "Time to come and help your gramma with supper."

There was only silence in response.

"You hear me, girl?"

"Yes, Uncle Ned," came Matty's slow reply.

"You come on down before it gets too dark," he called. "We don't want you lighting any candles up here. And don't you dawdle, now."

"All right," Matty sighed, "I just need to pack up my sewing." She sat still, listening to the fading sound of Ned's footsteps as he left the storage room and headed back down stairs. Repacking the round sewing basket and making certain all the cloth ends were well tucked in, she stood up and walked over to the opening of the cupola stairs. Leaning over, she took careful aim and dropped the basket. It bumped on the first turn of the steps and then rolled on down to the

storage room below without loosing any of its contents.

"Did it again," she laughed, then scrambled down the steps after it.

Chapter Two

$\mathcal{I}$n the dim light from the storage room window, Matty saw a small shape hump itself up from a pile of old draperies.

"Mmraaw. Mmraaw," it called out.

"So that's where you've been hiding, old Mr. Gray." Matty reached out and gave the smoky gray cat an affectionate stroke, running her fingers from his moist nose clear out to the very tip of his bushy tail.

"Silly thing. You always sound like you have a sore throat. When are you going to learn to talk like a proper cat. Now you say, me-ow...me-ow," Matty enunciated clearly. Mr. Gray just kept on purring, ignoring his teacher's instructions.

Gathering the cat into her arms, the girl looked wistfully around at the jumble of old furniture and several huge trunks full of the Warrens' unwanted goods. She loved being in this attic room. It was a feast for her lively imagination, all those reminders of days long ago when, according to Gramma Bess, the mansion was the scene of extravagant parties, musical entertainments, and formal meetings of the governor and his council.

A few times Matty had given in to temptation, lifting trunk lids to explore their contents. She marveled at arrays of fine, seemingly new clothes. Beneath muslin wrappings were delicate baby dresses and bonnets, lots of men's clothing including brightly colored silk waistcoats embroidered with gold thread. And, there were ladies' beautiful gowns, dozens of them, all carefully packed away.

Once, Matty had even been so bold as to lift out the upper part of a pink taffeta gown embroidered here and there with tiny lavender roses. Lovingly, she held it up against herself before a large cracked looking glass, then danced about the dusty room, delighting in the fabric's whispering swish. How she longed for the day when she would wear such lovely clothes, when she would finally live in that wonderful new

belonging place her father promised to find.

Now, with the snow storm still howling round about the mansion, Matty stood peering into that same looking glass. This time, however, it reflected only her tall, thin self, dressed in dull-colored work clothes. She studied her face, admiring long, silky lashes and clear, firm skin.

"Child," she recalled Bess saying one day, "you're getting to be the image of your dear mama, God rest her soul."

"Tell me again what she looked like," Matty had asked.

"Your mama Matilda, she was tall and delicate-boned and she had a lovely, welcoming face with big brown eyes and a smile that made your heart glad...just like you do."

"And," Ned spoke up, "your mama had that neat little rounded chin, same as you do, Missy."

"That chin got Matilda into trouble with Mrs. Warren sometimes," said Bess, "her holding it up so high. It don't do to go about with a bold face among white folks. They expect us to keep our eyes cast down, no matter what we're thinking. And you best remember that child."

Matty recalled nodding her head and then, after a while, quietly asking, "was it my fault, Gramma, that Mama died when I was born?"

"Oh, child, no...not at all. Sometimes birthing just don't go right. It's not anyone's fault. You mustn't fret yourself about that."

———✠———

Matty now turned away from that looking glass, bringing her thoughts back to the present. She heard the clock on the downstairs landing strike the hour of four. Picking up her sewing basket and settling Mr. Gray further under her arm, she headed for the storeroom door. "Come on, friend, we're wanted downstairs."

The girl descended a plain, enclosed staircase to a second floor landing and then paused to listen at the closed door of a bedchamber belonging to Mrs. Warren. As she expected, there was no sound from within. Poor old thing, Matty thought, she's probably just sitting in there staring out the window. Must be awful, her being shut away in that room all the time and nobody to keep her company.

Instead of continuing on down the servants' back staircase, Matty lifted the latch on a small door to her right and stepped out into a spacious hallway at the top of the mansion's grand staircase.

"I can use these stairs if I want to," she whispered. "Ain't nobody around says I can't."

She glanced defiantly at several portraits of the Warren family's stern-looking ancestors. In their heavily carved, gilded frames, they dominated the wall spaces between three other closed bedchamber doors. Except for Mrs. Warren, there was no one else to occupy those bedchambers. Nor had there been for many years. As for Mr. Warren, his weakening heart and aging knees had forced him to take up residence downstairs in the west parlor.

For the moment, with every door, upstairs and down, tightly closed against cold drafts, Matty's ears encountered only silence. Her nose, however, once it got past the ever-present smell of fireplace wood smoke, was treated to mouth-watering aromas drifting upward from Bess's kitchen.

Turning her back on those staring portraits, Matty beheld her most beloved sight in the entire mansion. Just

below her, at the mid-stair landing, was a great arched window and on either side of it were colorful paintings of larger-than-life Indians.

Hurrying down the short flight of steps, she set her basket down on a wide window seat. Mr. Gray, annoyed with being held, jumped from his mistress's arms to land on the seat. In bored cat fashion, he set about smoothing his rumpled fur with a busy pink tongue.

"Good afternoon, friends," Matty whispered, looking up to admire the tall Indians with their bold, dark-skinned faces, large piercing eyes and regal bearing. Each man was dressed in a short tunic adorned with tribal regalia and over broad shoulders was draped a long, flowing cape — red on one man, blue on the other. Above their heads and spanning the top of the arched window was painted a royal canopy with gold edging. Matty always felt a thrill at the sight of them, at least she had, once she got over her early childhood fear.

She smiled now at the memory, seeing herself as that tearful three-year old, discovering the Indians for the first time. There she was down at the bottom of the stairs that afternoon, hiding behind her grandmother's skirts and bawling at the top of her lungs. Mr. Warren had come hurrying out of the parlor to see what the commotion was all about. But he just laughed and then picked her up, gently carrying her up the steps for a closer look.

"Little One, you have nothing to fear from paintings on the wall," he said. "They're just pictures of good, brave men — Indian Kings — who went far across the sea to England a long time ago. And, they were guests of Queen Anne, too."

Despite Mr. Warren's efforts, Matty remembered that it took her quite a while before she could look at those Indians without shuddering. She had avoided them by insisting she would only use the servants stairway. But soon, her grandmother assigned her the weekly chore of dusting the grand staircase.

"You're not too young to take on a few small chores around here," Bess told her.

At first, the three year-old had quickly scurried a mop here and there over the steps, then run her dust rag along the banisters and in and around each of numerous carved spindles. All the while she tried to keep from glancing at the paintings above her. Eventually though, curiosity overcame fear.

"What a silly little goose I was," Matty now whispered, reaching up to brush her fingers lightly over the painted foot of the Indian in the red cape. She felt a comforting reassurance whenever in the presence of these figures, a kinship with people whose skin resembled her own. They did important things in the world, she often told herself, and someday I will, too.

For Matty, this lovely art work, like the rest of the beautifully furnished mansion, was a source of daily pleasure in her limited, isolated existence. Unaware, until recently, of her family's real situation in the Warren household, her child's heart had long ago claimed the house as her own.

"We're going into our other house," she used to inform her father and Uncle Ned as she happily toddled after Bess from their house into the mansion. Under Bess's watchful, but gentle attention, little Matty took delight in discovering her small shares of the household routine. Bess sometimes made a game of the work. When they were dusting the parlor furniture, she would say, "my old back don't work so good, child, so you're in charge of the under parts of things." Matty would gleefully crawl under tables and over chair rungs, dragging her dust rag while playing peek-a-boo with her grandmother.

During those earliest years, the tot seldom encountered the elderly Warrens and when she did, they seemed to her like distant, but kindly figures at the edges of her world. Visitors rarely came to the mansion and no longer were there any grand entertainments and meetings of government officials.

Now, in the gathering darkness of this December afternoon of 1806, Matty stood looking up at the paintings with a keen feeling of loss. Gramma's stories have spoiled everything for me, she thought, — this beautiful mansion, the Warrens and even Portsmouth.

As if to escape from her feelings, Matty grabbed her sewing basket and hurried down to the first floor. Carefully, she tiptoed past Mr. Warren's closed parlor door. Even through the heavy panel, she could hear the man snoring away.

Rounding the newel post, she headed into the darkness of the back hall and was just about to enter the kitchen when she heard Bess and Ned's loud voices. Clearly, an argument was going on. Instead of lifting the iron latch on the door, Matty quietly stepped back into a corner and crouched down to listen. Her cat began rubbing back and forth against her ankles as if to ask, why are we stopping in this cold, drafty hallway when there's a warm kitchen waiting?

"I've done the best I know how for that child." Bess's complaining voice reached Matty's ears.

"Of course you have," came Ned's reply, " but it won't do no good to be so short with her."

"But she's become such a dawdler, moping around this house all the time. And her work's getting sloppy." Bess paused. Then she asked, " You did call her down here, didn't you, Ned?"

"Of course I did."

"Well, what's taking her so long?" Bess's voice rose in annoyance.

"She'll be along, Sister. Don't fret yourself. Our Matty will be coming through that door any minute now."

Matty clamped a hand over her mouth, suppressing a giggle.

For a moment or two, all she heard beyond the door was a snapping, crackling sound of wood burning in the fireplace and then a soft, repeated thumping. Gramma is probably rolling out pie dough, she guessed.

"Can't you settle that fire down a bit?" Bess called to her brother. "Push those logs back further into the fireplace so the downdraft can't keep shooting sparks out onto the floor. I wish this snow storm would let up."

"Don't go telling me how to tend a fire," Ned growled.

At that, the thumping sound grew louder and a bit faster. Then Bess spoke up again. "What are we going to do about Matty, Ned? After all we've told her, her head is still so full of her father's impossible dreams."

"I sure know that," replied Ned. "You should hear the fanciful stories she chatters on about when the two of us are working round the place...all that talk about us going away to live in a big, new house her papa's going to buy... and her going to school and traveling and..."

"You must put a stop to such foolishness," Bess interrupted.

"I don't have the heart to," he said. "She needs to talk to somebody."

"That can't go on, Ned. She's got to understand what we've been telling her, the dangers for African people. Freedom is not what she thinks it is. It's way past time for her to settle down and face reality."

"Well, she sure got a good load of reality from your stories," said Ned.

"It was your idea to tell her about the family and all," replied Bess. "You said we ought to do it before another Christmas comes around."

"I just thought you'd kinda explain things sorta general like, not put such a powerful load of stuff on her shoulders so quick. And anyway," he said, " you shoulda been telling her small bits about all that long before now. And, you shoulda been lettin' her out of this house more...let her go visiting with other African children so she'd get to know about our situation and all. Why, she's been like a prisoner here since Peter left."

"Ned, that's not true! She's always gone about the town with us, shopping and such. And, she goes up the hill to St.

John's Church with us every Sunday."

The woman's voice sounded close to tears. "You know I've just been trying to keep her safe until Peter came... er,...comes back for her. What if she got stolen away by some slaver?" Bess's voice cracked in distress.

Matty felt awful, hearing her grandmother cry. She started moving toward the kitchen door and then stopped when she heard Ned speak up.

"Aw, Sister, I'm sorry. I didn't mean to get you upset. Everything's going to come out right. We just got to keep a steady head. And, you know, Bess, miracles do happen. Peter might still come back."

"Oh, I want to keep hoping, but it's so hard," said Bess. "You know what I went through after my husband went away... all those awful years of waiting. Only God knows what happened to him or where he might be... if he's even still alive."

Matty couldn't stand hearing more. Quickly, she lifted the latch and entered the kitchen, waiting only a moment for the cat to slink past her before closing the door.

"Are you making apple pies, Gramma?" Matty put on a big smile as she came to stand beside Bess's cluttered work table in the middle of the large candle-lit room.

"No, I'm going to make meat pies." Bess hastily pulled off her spectacles and dabbed at her eyes with a corner of her apron. Settling the glasses back on her nose, she gave Matty a stern look. "And, what took you so long getting down here, I want to know. Probably got lost in your silly daydreaming, I'll wager."

Matty merely shrugged, then headed for the warmth

of the big open fireplace just as Mr. Gray had done.

"Oh well," said Ned, trying to lighten the atmosphere, "our Matty's here now so we best get on with the work." He took a heavy black coat off a wall peg and shrugged into it. Worn and patched at the elbows, that hand-me-down coat had seen better days when Mr. Warren wore it.

"Looks like the snow's pretty much stopped," he said, "so I'll go shovel a path to the carriage barn and then milk the cow before she gets too cranky." He reached out and patted Matty on the shoulder, then headed out through the pantry to the back yard.

An uncomfortable silence followed in the wake of Ned's departure. Bess continued shaping dough for three large pies. When finished, she would put the unfilled crusts out in the pantry, until Ned fired up the bake oven in the morning.

Matty remained hunkered down on the wide brick hearth in front of the deep fireplace. Her long skirts were carefully tucked up and wrapped closely about her knees. She was well aware of the danger of flying sparks, how easily and quickly they could ignite the cotton cloth.

She glanced about at various cooking operations under way. On her left, two chickens were roasting in a tin reflector oven, their savory drippings sizzled and sputtered in the pan below. Over the fire, on a long iron crane, were suspended two small kettles and a large water cauldron, their contents simmering away. Now and then, they whispered softly to one another as lids lifted in huffs of steam.

"Gramma," Matty spoke up quietly, not turning around, "what if Papa never comes back for me? What will I do? Where will I belong?"

"Oh, dear child," said Bess, rubbing more flour on her rolling pin, "you have no need to worry your head about that. You will always have a home with Ned and me. You'll belong in Portsmouth with us."

"But Papa said we don't belong here and we need to —"

"Now you stop your talk about such things, Matty. We are, all of us, just where the good Lord set us down. We got to be accepting and make the best of that."

"But Gramma—"

"We haven't got time for all that now," Bess interrupted again. "You just come along and set up the Warrens' supper trays. And, mind how you fold those clean linen napkins. I want to see corners matched neat and straight."

"Yes, Gramma." Matty stood up and stretched herself, then walked reluctantly toward a service cupboard located at the opposite end of the kitchen. On the way, she dragged her fingers aimlessly over the stained, well-worn surface of another work table against the wall. She often stood there peeling vegetables or washing the Warren's dishes. Next, she brushed imaginary dust off the upper panel of a small closed door. Behind it was concealed the servants' narrow back passageway which lead to Mr. Warren's front parlor. Upon finally reaching the service cupboard, Matty began taking down plates and cups from shelves above it.

"Have a care, mind you, with those delicate china cups," cautioned Bess. "If you break any more, Mr. Warren is sure to take it out of our wages."

At least he won't take a whip to us the way people did to my ancestors, Matty wanted to shout, but didn't. Her angry thought had risen unexpected. It sent a sickish feeling deep into her stomach. It's all Gramma's fault, she thought. Why did she have to tell me all those awful stories.

Chapter Three

*M*atty would never forget that evening, two weeks before, when her view of the world turned frightening. And, when her dreams of a happy future began to fade.

Throughout that workday, she had noticed something different about her relatives' behavior. Both of them were unusually quiet and sort of distant. Whenever she tried asking what was wrong, they put off answering.

"Stop pestering us," Bess finally said as they stood in the mansion kitchen. "We'll talk about it after supper. You just go set the table in our house. Ned and I will be along with the food soon."

Later, in their candle-lit "everything" room, the mood of that day continued right on through their supper. Instead of the family's usual light-hearted chatter, they ate in near silence. Even Mr. Gray, curled on Matty's lap, seemed to sense the change in mood. He lay perfectly still, forgoing his habit of begging for scraps. By the end of the meal, Matty was certain that something was terribly wrong.

"Have you heard from Papa — has there been any letter yet?," she asked, dreading bad news.

"No. No letter," Bess sighed, getting up from the table. "There's been no news of him, child."

Matty began to cry. "Gramma, please tell me what's wrong."

"Nothing's really wrong," said Ned. "We just need to explain some things to you about — "

"We will talk about it later," Bess quickly interrupted,

"when we get back from settling down the Warrens for the night. Meantime, you just see to the dishes."

＊＊＊

"Why do I always get stuck with the dishes," Matty grumbled to a now empty room. She stood up, dumping the cat to the floor. "Some day, when Papa and I have lots of money, I'm gonna throw out the dirty dishes after every meal and I'll buy new ones. And I'll hire a servant to do the cooking so Gramma won't have to."

Smiling to herself, she proceeded to scrape leftovers into a wooden slop bucket, then she put two tin wash basins up on the table and partly filled them with hot water from their fireplace cauldron before adding some cold. Grabbing a chunk of rock-hard lye soap, she plunged her winter-chapped hands into one of the basins and tried to rub up a bit of lather.

"It'd be nice if cats could dry the dishes." She flicked a few drops of water down at Mr. Gray. "Your bushy tail ought to do the job."

＊＊＊

It seldom took long for Bess and Ned to attend to the Warrens' nightly care. He usually finished his duties before she did. According to Ned, old Mr. Warren wasn't one to tolerate much fussing about himself. There'd be a brief wash-up of face and hands, then Ned would help the elderly man into night clothes and settle him into bed. Mr. Warren was fussy about his slippers, though. He never failed to remind Ned to line them up at a particular spot under the side of the bed so if he needed them in the night, his bare feet wouldn't have to touch the cold floor.

Before bidding his employer good night, Ned would see to it that the inside shutters were tightly closed against the cold, then put a few more logs on the fire. And, if need be, he would replace a soiled chamber pot with an empty one. Should Mr. Warren require anything during the night, he could just pull on a cord which ran back through the walls to a bell in his servants' quarters.

As for Mrs. Warren's care, Matty knew that would keep her grandmother away a bit longer. A severe stroke seven years ago left Caroline Warren without speech, a partly paralyzed arm and growing mental confusion. That once proud, beautiful and demanding woman now stared at the world with vacant eyes while her former slave patiently attended to her extensive needs.

Before leaving, Bess always made certain that the burning logs and hot ash in the fireplace were pushed far back into the brick recess. Then she would put a pierced tin screen in front of it, latching it securely in place. Matty's father made that clever device after Mrs. Warren's stroke so that the woman would be protected from accidentally tumbling into the fire.

A bell-pull cord was located close to the head of Mrs Warren's bed so, if need be, she could summon Bess's help during the night. In times gone by, when Bess was still held in slavery, she would have been expected to stay over night, sleeping on a floor mat near the ill woman's bed. No doubt Bess was grateful she no longer was forced to do that.

"Now then, Mistress Matty," said Bess, finally rejoining her granddaughter, "we'll have our bit of time together. I'm sorry you've had to wait so long."

Putting her arm around the girl, she walked her over to the settle and they sat down facing the fireplace. Ned came around the other end of the old worn bench, placing himself close beside his grand niece. Matty gave him a big smile and a share of their lap robe. She felt warm and cozy being nestled between her relatives.

Behind the family, the rest of the room was chilly, but in front, a blazing log fire played with their comfort. It gave generously of its heat, but now and then, it encouraged cold drafts to sneak under, around and over the tall-backed bench before drawing them up the chimney.

Bess reached out and gently took Matty's hand, drawing it across her lap.

"Matty, there are some things we must talk to you about, things you're old enough to understand now. You remember when we got our freedom papers, don't you, just before your Papa left, and his talk of our ancestors being brought here as slaves?"

Matty nodded, looking up into her grandmother's eyes.

"Well, we need to explain more about that and our situation here with the Warrens and...with other white people."

"You do know what a slave is, don't you," Ned asked Matty.

"It's somebody who doesn't have their freedom paper yet," she piped up, " so they can't go anywhere they want to."

"It's a lot more than that, I can tell you." Ned tossed his head in disgust.

"Ned, please let me do the talking," said Bess. "We agreed that I would be the one to tell the child about all this." Bess pulled her shawl up around herself, trying to compose her thoughts.

"Our parents," she began, "they grew up as slaves on a big sugar plantation on the island of Barbados far south of here in the West Indies. They lived among hundreds of other Africans who were forced to work, most of them, in the cane fields. Others had to work at the plantation house and look after the white people who owned them."

"Owned them?" Matty interrupted. "I don't

understand. You mean they owned your parents — same as furniture, or clothes and such?"

"Yes, they did"

"Did they buy them in a store?" Matty asked in astonishment.

"No, child, of course not. Now you just be still for a while and listen to what I'm trying to say. You'll understand, soon enough.

"Momma and Papa's parents were among the many, many thousands of African people who were captured and sold to slave traders. Then they were put in chains and herded onto ships that brought them to America."

"God awful thing to do to human beings," Ned muttered.

"Our parents never got a chance to know their folks," Bess went on, "because, not long after they were born, each baby's set of parents was taken away and sold to a plantation owner on another island. It was a dreadful mean thing to do, something that happened now and then on those plantations. Slave owners cared nothing for Africans' feelings or for their families, just the money from the sales.

"Each baby was given to a different woman who raised it with her own children. Mama was named Taba and the family who took in Papa, they called him Jube. We think those were African names, but we're not sure.

"Mama didn't tell us much about her substitute mother, except to say she was mostly kind. The woman was strict, though, making sure Mama learned her work in the plantation house in the proper way and did whatever the white people told her to. She didn't want Mama getting beaten or whipped by the master or his overseer."

"We don't know much of anything about Papa's substitute family," Ned put in, "or his growing up. He just wasn't a talker."

"No," said Bess. "Mama was always the story teller, when the mood took her. And she certainly could make stories interesting. Of course she didn't share the real bad ones with us 'til we were older — all those awful things that happened on the plantation and their coming to Portsmouth. Early on, she'd just settle us kids to sleep with happy stories, ones she'd heard about Africa; the strange animals and about life in villages where kings and queens ruled. You know, Matty, the stories I used to tell you when—"

"Come on, Bess," Ned interrupted, "don't get off the path. Get on with telling the child what she needs to know."

"Gramma," Matty suddenly pulled on Bess's arm. "Why did they do that?"

"Do what, child?"

"Why did they capture African people — make them slaves?"

"Because there wasn't anyone to stop them. No laws against it," Bess replied.

"It was greed!" Ned pounded the arm of the bench. "...rotten greed for money and free labor. And, the law in this country still lets them do it."

"Please, Ned," said Bess, "let me tell it my way."

"Anyway," she continued, "our Mama was sixteen or thereabouts — she never knew her birthday exactly — when she met Papa. And it wasn't a happy occasion. They saw one another for the first time down at the plantation wharf. They were among a group of six young boys and girls who had been sold to a sea captain from New Hampshire.

"Papa noticed Mama 'cause she was shaking and crying. He feared she might call attention to herself and get punished. The captain had a whip in his hand. So when the white man wasn't looking, Papa moved over next to her and quietly tried to comfort her.

"Once on board the ship, the young people were forced to climb down into a dark hold where barrels of molasses, sacks of rice and other cargo nearly filled the space. A trap door with a few small holes in it was then locked down over their heads. Inside that hold there was only a small space with close-together wooden shelves where the group was expected to live and sleep. Mama said it was a terrible place, not fit for people; so damp and airless and dirty. She got seasick almost immediately and stayed that way most of the time they were at sea. She said the only good thing about it was being near Papa and his giving her a special name. He called her his Pretty Bird."

In her low, soothing voice, Bess continued telling her mother's story of the long, rough voyage north, of the young people's terror as to what lay ahead for them. She spoke of their arrival at the Portsmouth wharf one snowy morning in February of 1730 and of their being sold at auction. Now and then, Bess paused, perhaps searching for the right words and details she thought appropriate for young ears .

Matty took in every word with rapt attention. Staring straight ahead into the fireplace, into those glowing, ever-changing, hot caves beneath the burning logs, she could almost see it happening — even imagine herself there with her great grandparents, shivering in the cold winter wind while standing in deep snow.

How awful it must have been, she thought, that crowd of white people staring at them and their ragged clothing, rudely looking them over as if they weren't human beings with feelings.

"Mama and Papa had no idea where they were," said Bess, " and they hadn't ever seen a city like this before. It was all so frightening. Their biggest fear, though, was that they would be sold to different masters and never see one another again. They dearly wanted to stay together and become husband and wife.

"They were the last ones to be auctioned off, but the bidding was slow. Mama guessed it was because she and Papa had lost so much weight from terrible food and sea sickness. Finally, a short, fat man named Captain John McIntire told the auctioneer he would take them both for two pounds and six shillings and no one objected.

A clerk wrote Papa's name on the sale document and when Mama told him her name was Taba Pretty Bird, McIntire just laughed and told the clerk to write down the name 'Dinah', instead. Then he threw a horse blanket over their shoulders and walked them up the hill to this house."

"Papa told us he refused to call Mama by her slave name," said Ned. "We always heard him call her 'Pretty Bird' or just 'Pretty'."

"What happened to the other young people, Gramma? Were they sent to the plantations?"

"No, no. There weren't any plantations around here. Likely, they were put to work in other mansion houses in

Portsmouth or sent out to the farms."

"I recall Papa saying they were terrible lonesome at first," said Ned, "because there weren't many Africans here then, not more than about fifty. And so scattered around the town, they seldom saw one another. None of them was free, as far as he knew. He said, bad as that Barbados plantation was, at least there they had the comfort of friends near by."

"Why did my great grandparents stay here? Why didn't they just run away? I would have."

"Matty, you don't know what you're talking about," Ned growled. "It was dangerous. They couldn't just run off."

There was a moment of silence. Then Matty asked, "Gramma, were there white people who were slaves in Portsmouth?"

"No, not that I ever heard of. Just African people."

"But why just African people? I don't understand." Matty shook her head in frustration.

"There ain't no UNDERSTANDING about it," Ned burst out. "Slavery is just wrong! Plain wrong!"

"Ned, Matty — stop it," Bess intervened. "This is getting out of hand. Matty, you've got to be patient and hold back on your questions for a while. There's so much to be explained to you, but it can't all be done in a rush.

"Anyway, we should stop now. It's late. Let's have our Bible reading and prayers. Tomorrow night, Matty, we'll tell you more about the family and about your papa."

Long into that mid-December night, the first of Bess's stories, Matty recalled that her mind refused to settle into sleep. With her nightcap pulled down over her ears and wool covers up to her chin, she lay in her narrow trundle bed, staring into the darkness. She tried not to toss about on the straw-filled mattress for fear of waking her grandmother in the bed next to hers. Bess's wheezy, soft snores kept steady company with her brother's louder ones. His could be heard coming from beyond the wooden partition which separated the two second floor rooms.

Slave...slavery..., Matty thought. Those were just words. I've heard them before, but I never thought about what they really meant. Now I know. She shuddered at the realization. We used to be *SLAVES*. Mr. Warren *OWNED* us.

Oh, I got to stop thinking about that. Got to think about something pleasant or I'll never get to sleep.

But escape didn't come so easily. Instead, scenes and conversations from her own past came swirling about in her head, demanding attention. Scenes of when she first discovered a puzzling difference between herself and white people, something more than just skin color. She saw herself at about age five, not long after her father went away, happily trooping along beside her grandmother for shopping and other errands. She remembered smiling up every passerby. The few Africans they met along the way always smiled in return, sometimes stopping to pat her head and chat a bit. But she soon noticed that white people mostly ignored her or sometimes gave her unkind looks. If she tried making friends with their children, the parents pulled them away, often telling them 'don't bother with those Negroes'.

The first time that happened, she piped up loudly, "Gramma, why did they do that — pull their children away from me?"

"Oh, come along, child," Bess said quietly. " Don't fret yourself about that."

"But Gramma, what's wrong? Why — "

"Matty, not now. Later, when you are older, I'll explain about all that."

And there had been that day long ago when a neighbor's young visitor was sitting on the back yard fence making faces at her while Bess was hanging up the laundry.

"You ain't nothing," he called out. "You're just old Negro slaves!"

Matty recalled being frightened and her grandmother hurrying her into the house. But afterward, no one was willing to explain to her what that was all about.

As she grew older, she tried questioning Uncle Ned about such incidents and about other things such as her not going to school like the white children did, why she didn't have their pretty clothes and ride in fancy carriages, why she and other African people were not allowed to sit in the first floor pews at church. But Ned just shrugged his shoulders or gave the same vague replies that Bess always did. Eventually, she gave up asking questions.

Well, Matty now thought as her eyelids grew heavy, at least I'm getting some answers about all that. But, I still can't make any sense out of why white people would treat African folks in such mean and terrible ways.

Oh, come on, she silently scolded herself, no sense going over and over Gramma's stories and that old, by-gone stuff. That's really got nothing to do with me, now.

She turned on her side, pulling the covers nearly over

her head.　Soon as my papa comes back, she thought, we'll leave all that slave stuff behind.　Won't be none of that in our new belonging place.

Does seem strange, though, Gramma and Uncle Ned wanting to tell me about it right now.　And why were they acting so upset about doing it?

Chapter Four

$\mathcal{A}$s Matty recalled, the next day was a long and frustrating one. She kept trying to question Bess and Ned, wanting to hear more about the family. But each time they put her off. "Keep your questions in your head 'til later, child" was all she heard. When "later" finally came that evening, she remembered curling up on the settle feeling relieved but a bit anxious.

"I've been thinking about our talk last night, Matty." Bess put another log on the fire before sitting down beside her. "...about what you said, thinking your great grandparents ought to have run away. It just couldn't be that way, not if they hoped to stay together and be safe.

"I don't think you can imagine how fearful they were about coming here, about their new master and what might happen to them in the future. And, how awful it was being forced to work day in and day out, just the two of them, caring for that big mansion, the constant cooking, cleaning, hauling water from the well and keeping the fireplaces going. Sometimes, when the house was full of company, there might be as many as eleven fireplaces to keep going, plus attending to the demands of all those extra people.

"And there were the animals in the carriage barn, the vegetable garden, and doing any other work that the Captain and his wife required. The only time our parents had to themselves was the few hours' sleep they got at night."

"You think we work hard, Matty," Ned spoke up, "but that's nothing compared to then. And we got some say in the matter now that we're free and on hire. Our folks sure didn't."

A tapping sound could be heard coming from behind the settle. Ned had chosen not to join them that evening. Instead, he was sitting at his work-cluttered end of their long pine table, replacing three brass sleigh bells which had been lost from the horse's harness. Now and then, he whistled softly to himself.

"Guess Mama had a worse time at first than Papa did," Bess continued. "She was mostly confined to the mansion property, except on Sundays when she and Papa were forced to attend the North Congregational Meetinghouse with the McIntires. Well, not with them. They had to sit up in the gallery with other Africans, same as we do now at St. John's Church.

"Papa, now, he got to go on errands around town and, after he learned to drive the Captain's horse and carriage, he got to see some of the sights when he took the McIntires around about Portsmouth. He even drove the Captain on trips up country and down to Boston and other places in Massachusetts."

" Mama told us that during those first few months after they came here, she was so scared and so bone cold that if it hadn't been for Papa, she would have just turned up her toes and died. But he kept her going, giving her courage. Sometimes he did whisper to her in the night about their running away, but each time Mama begged him not to even think about it. She was sure they'd be caught. She remembered seeing some terrible whippings of captured runaways at the Barbados plantation. Captain McIntire had a whip. It hung coiled up on a peg in the back hallway of the mansion, over the fire buckets."

"Did — did the Captain ever use that whip on your parents?" Matty asked fearfully.

"We don't know," replied Bess. "He may have."

"I tried asking Papa about that a couple of times," Ned called out, " but he wouldn't answer me. Just told me to do my work and mind my business."

"Did you or Uncle Ned ever get —"

"No, child, never." Bess gave her a reassuring pat on the knee. "But that whip did stay in the hallway for many, many years." For a few moments, Bess stared thoughtfully at the glowing fireplace before resuming.

"Mama said once that, when she looked back on her life, it just seemed like so much gray dishwater with just a few nice bubbles in it — us kids. But she also said that when we were little, she and Papa lived in constant fear something bad might happen to us 'bubbles'."

"Fun being thought of as a bubble," laughed Matty. "But why were your folks so scared, Gramma?"

"In those days, families lost a lot of babies and little ones — white as well as African. Awful diseases and infections and the nasty cold winters sometimes took them off to the burial ground before their time. African folks, though, they had another kind of worry about losing their children.

"First time Mama and Papa knew they were going to have a baby, they wanted so much to be happy about that, but they felt uneasy. They never got over what happened to them as babies on the plantation, having their parents sold away. And, they knew also that slave owners sometimes would wait until a child grew old enough to work, about six or seven years old, then they'd sell it away from the parents. Our folks didn't know if the Captain would ever do that, but they always prayed hard that he wouldn't."

"I'm sure glad nothing bad ever happened to you and Uncle Ned." Despite her words, Matty's voice sounded a bit shaky and she gripped her grandmother's hand.

"No, we survived just fine, Matty. I am sorry to tell you that the folks lost that first baby to an infection before it was a month old. Then, it wasn't until nearly ten years later, in 1746 that Ned and I were born."

"To hear Papa tell it," said Ned, " the McIntires were so pleased with our arrival, you might have thought we were their children — the ones they never had. The Captain chose our names and took a lively interest in our upbringing. He insisted we learn to talk proper English. Later he and Mrs. McIntire taught us some reading and writing and a bit of figuring, too. Mama said she wondered about such learning because, as far she knew, that was unusual for slaves. The McIntires never taught her and Papa such things."

"Anyway," Bess resumed the story, " Papa thought our learning was a good thing, but Mama, she was suspicious of what the Captain might be planning. Africans who had such special learning often sold for a higher price at auctions.

"Of course, as it turned out, he wasn't planning anything," Bess said. We just grew up, working around here same as Mama and Papa did. Papa sometimes teased us for talking better English than he and Mama did, but I think he was proud of us just the same.

"Ned and I were seventeen years old when Captain McIntire died. His ship went down in a sudden spring storm when he was returning from Ireland. As a result, the mansion and all his property — including our family, mind you — was willed to his nephew, Joshua Warren. Mrs. McIntire went to live with her sister in Salem."

"The Captain's dying was scary news for us," Ned piped up. "Papa said that the new master might decide to break up our family, sell some of us away. He talked about us running off before that happened. He told Mama there was a good chance we could make it to safety. You see, he heard rumors about some Africans from Portsmouth who escaped and were thought to be living out west with friendly Indian tribes."

"Gosh, I'd like that, Uncle Ned. Why don't we go out there? I'd love to meet the Indians."

"Oh, hush, child," said Bess, "You know that's not possible. Now let me keep on with the story.

"Actually, Papa was thinking seriously about going west before the new master arrived, but then Mama got real sick. Her lungs had been bothering her for quite a while and she had a terrible cough — probably from all that cooking smoke and ash we all breathe. Anyhow, she suddenly got much worse. Papa doubted she'd survive a long journey and he wasn't about to leave her behind. So we stayed.

"Mama said not to worry. Like always, she kept telling us, 'mind you just do your work, don't make trouble and, God willing, we'll be safe'.

"It was kinda like a hurricane when those Warrens moved in, wasn't it, Bess," Ned called out.

"It surely was," Bess replied. "That snooty Mrs. Warren and her daughter, Hannah, they stormed in here, determined to change everything about the mansion. Nothing the

McIntires had was good enough for them. We had to move all
the Captain's furniture up to the storage room so the Warrens
could buy new. And, when their barrels of fancy china dishes
arrived from England, they told us to smash the McIntires'
china and put it down the privy hole.

"That nice green teapot and its cream pitcher, Matty,
the ones we use all the time, I saved them from going down
the privy when no one was looking. Hid them under my bed
for years."

Matty giggled.

"Remember, Bess, how we had to wash down the
whole mansion," said Ned, " — the walls, windows, floors —
and the place just wasn't that dirty. I can still hear Papa
muttering about 'those crazy women'. For months, the Mrs.
and her daughter had painters, wallpaper hangers and carpen-
ters traipsing around the place. Wasn't much they didn't fancy
up. And, Mr. Warren, he just stood back and paid the bills."

"Well — ," Bess gave a slow smile, "there was one thing
Mrs. Caroline Warren didn't get her way about. She didn't like
the paintings on the grand staircase, Matty. You see, there used
to be more of them on the walls on either side of the Indians,
scenes of animals and white people. Well, you should have
heard the screaming and shouting that went on because Mr.
Warren wouldn't let her have all the paintings covered over
with wallpaper. He told her he liked those Indian Kings and
he wouldn't have them covered. And that was that."

"I'm awful glad he saved those Indians, Gramma."

"Yes, but that battle was unusual for him. He let his
wife have her way about most everything else."

Bess and Ned went on talking about those difficult

early years, the increasing amount of work expected of them as the Warrens set about making their mark on Portsmouth society. But, it began to seem to Matty as though the elderly twins were talking to each other rather than to her.

Wish I could just go to bed now, she thought, not have to hear any more of that slave stuff. I'll probably have nightmares thinking about people being whipped, babies dying and little children being sold away from their parents. Don't know what awful thing they're going to be telling me next.

Reluctantly, she made herself listen while more stories were told about the Warrens' constant entertaining of visitors, their large dinner parties with dancing late into the night and Mrs. Warren's lavish afternoon tea parties. She heard about Joshua Warren being a member of the King's colonial council and his ambition for becoming governor.

Bess and Ned told about all the work involved in Hannah's wedding celebrations before she sailed away to live in France. They spoke of the many Warren relatives and friends who often crowded into the mansion's extra bedchambers, bringing along personal maids and numerous heavy trunks. Their stays often lasted for weeks or even months.

According to Bess, all of that was a steady, exhausting, dawn-to-midnight load of work for the enslaved family. For Taba Pretty Bird, it eventually proved too much. She collapsed in the mansion kitchen one evening and was gone before morning. Her family was allowed to attend her burial on the Warrens' farm a few miles up river in Newington, but there was not much ceremony about it. A few days afterward, Mr. Warren went to his mother's house in Salem, Massachusetts, and brought back a tall, twenty-four-year-old enslaved African named Pompi.

"That Pompi, he sure brought the sunshine with him," Matty heard Ned say. "He was just what we needed, especially for your grandma, wasn't he, Bess." Ned chuckled as he put aside his work and came around to join them on the settle.

"Oh, Ned. None of your teasing, now." Bess pretended to be cross, then she smiled at Matty. "I wish you could have known my handsome Pompi. He was such a dear man, a breath of fresh air…so light-hearted and friendly…and curious about everything. He brought a few books with him when he first came here and sometimes he'd read to us in the evening. I didn't understand even half of it — all that philosophy stuff — but I loved being near him and hearing his deep voice.

"He behaved so different around Mr. Warren, too. Never hesitated to speak right up to him. Of course he was always polite, but the two of them used to get into the darnedest discussions about all manner of things. Several times I heard Mrs. Warren voicing her disapproval that her husband was on such friendly terms with a 'Negro'. But the Mister seemed to pay her no mind."

"Tell her about your wedding, Bess." Ned grinned and poked Matty with his elbow. "Pompi told me he had it in his mind to propose the first time he saw her."

Matty watched as her grandmother rubbed at a worn brass ring she always wore on her left hand. It dug into her fat finger.

"We had to get Mr. Warren's permission," Bess explained, "and then, one Sunday afternoon in 1768, after the second church service, Mr. Warren asked the minister to perform the ceremony. Afterward, Mr. Warren told us we wouldn't have to go back to work. We could have the rest of the day to ourselves. I couldn't believe it."

"It was Pompi's doing," said Ned, " his being on such good terms with Mr. Warren. All of our lives took a turn for the better, Matty, after Pompi arrived."

"Yes, I guess if there was ever a really happy time for us," said Bess, "it was with Pompi. He and Ned were a great pair, too, laughing and joking. You would have thought they didn't have a care in the world and, they both loved to play tricks on people.

"Would you believe, Matty, there was one night when the two of them snuck into the Warrens' bedroom and they put a dead mouse under Mrs. Warren's fancy white wig, a tall one that she kept on a wooden stand on her dressing table.

"Next morning, you could hear that woman screaming clear out to our house. She was certain one of us had done it and told Mr. Warren to get out the whip. But, he just laughed and called Pompi to remove the mouse. Later, though, Mr. Warren did take him aside and warned him to make certain that nothing like that ever happened again."

"Wish I'd been there to see that," Matty laughed.

"It was my Pompi's doing that we got some extra time off each week, other than for Sunday church."

"Well, now," said Ned, sounding a bit annoyed, "don't you forget, Bess, I was with Pompi that morning when we went to talk with Mr. Warren about that."

"I know, but I don't think you ever would have if it hadn't been for Pompi's bold ways.

"Anyway, Matty," Bess continued, "it helped a lot to

know we could look forward to a few hours away from the mansion. Some afternoons Pompi and I would walk up Chapel hill to the burial ground and find a nice grassy spot to sit on. Then we'd look out over the river and all the great ships and he'd tell me about far-off places he'd heard of.

"Other times, we'd go for a short visit with friends in town. And, wherever Pompi went, people would flock around him, including some white men, gossiping and laughing, pumping him for whatever news he'd collected. At times, he was better than a newspaper.

"Sometimes, when we were walking around the table serving supper to the Warrens — and whoever else might be staying in the mansion — Pompi would just come out with some of the latest news he'd heard. And everyone at the table seemed to enjoy listening to him, except Mrs. Warren, of course. She'd keep shooting nasty looks at her husband and loudly clearing her throat. I didn't dare look at Ned for fear we'd both laugh out loud." Bess and Ned smiled at each other, enjoying the memory.

Least they had something to laugh about in those slave days, Matty thought.

"Anyway, child," Bess went on, "it was about six years later that your papa came into our lives, April 4, 1775. It was a wonderful time for us, but our happiness didn't last long before the worries set in."

"What was wrong Gramma? Was my Papa a sickly baby?"

"No, not at all. He was a fine, healthy boy. It was the war that started causing trouble for us, my Pompi getting himself mixed in with the politics. If he hadn't, he would still be with us. You would have gotten to know your grandpa."

"He was doing the right thing, Bess. We all were," said Ned.

"What happened to him?" Matty turned so she could look Ned full in the face.

He and Bess exchanged glances over Matty's head. They had finally come to one of the main reasons for telling her their sometimes rambling story. They seemed uncertain as to who should speak next.

Bess heaved a sigh. "Well, for years, Pompi had been paying close attention to all the political commotion going on in the colonies, their quarreling with the British king over new laws and him sending more British soldiers over here. Pompi heard lots about all that whenever he drove Mr. Warren's carriage to Boston and elsewhere. Then, when the colonies declared their independence in 1776, Pompi and other Africans in Portsmouth started looking for ways to get our freedom. And, it did look like that just might be possible.

" By then, you see, things had begun changing for us around here. For one thing, there were a lot more Africans in Portsmouth than when our parents were first brought here, maybe as many as a hundred. Most of us were still held in slavery, but we were allowed to go around town more on our own, visiting and attending bigger social gatherings of our people."

"Yes, I sure enjoyed those gatherings," Ned spoke up. "We got to learn a lot more about Africa, the old ways and the stories and songs. Sometimes we went to meetings of the African Court to watch to our elected officials settle disputes or order a whipping for thieves and such."

"Did they put people in jail, too?"

"No, they didn't, Matty," said Bess, leaning forward to look at her brother. "Ned, I'm getting weary of your interruptions. It's hard enough trying to keep my story straight so I don't forget something important.

"That court, Matty, it was set up by our people a few years before the revolutionary war started and we had a king in charge of it, just like back in Africa.

"Each June, on our election day, we'd get dressed up in our best clothes and join with all the other Africans for a parade out to the Plains on the edge of town. Then there'd be a coronation of our newly elected king and we'd have a great celebration, lasting all day. It was so grand. Made us feel proud. And, the white people didn't give us any trouble about it.

"Well, one October night, in 1779," Bess continued, "a few years after the war with England got going, Pompi stood up at a meeting of our African Court and, with their permission, he read them a copy of the Declaration of Independence, every word of it. When he finished, he told them that document meant everyone in America was free. And, that included Africans, too.

"A week or so later, he and your Uncle Ned and some other men wrote up a petition to the New Hampshire government saying that we had a right to be free. Pompi and the rest of the men

signed it and sent it by messenger to the state capitol in Exeter."

"Did my great grandpa Jube sign it, too?"

"Oh Matty, I wish so much he had still been with us to do that," Bess replied. "But, he was gone by then. Shortly after Peter was born, our papa died from falling off a ladder when they were repairing the mansion roof."

Matty leaned her head against her grandmother's shoulder, trying to give her a bit of comfort.

"After that freedom petition was sent off," Bess said, "it was more than six months before Pompi found out what happened to it. And, when he did, that was a terrible day for us.

"That June morning, he was serving coffee to the Warrens and their guest in the parlor — the west one, Matty, where old Mr. Warren sleeps now. That guest was a man from the New Hampshire government. According to Pompi, soon as the guest saw him come into the room with the tray, the man looked right at him and laughed. Then he told Mr. Warren, 'oh, by the way, that petition your Negroes sent us, it isn't going to do them any good. The State Assembly decided to just put the thing aside for a more *convenient* time. But I'm sure such a time will never come'.

"I was out in the kitchen that morning, waiting for Pompi to get back from serving. I couldn't figure out what was taking him so long. I walked inside that back passageway to the parlor and there he was, sitting on the floor, not making a sound, tears streaming down his face. It was shocking. I'd never seen him cry before. I got him out to the kitchen and he told me what happened."

Bess looked away, hastily drawing a handkerchief out of her pocket and trying to hide tears beginning to flow. Then she went on with her story.

"Late that same night, after everyone had gone to bed, Pompi bundled up some clothing and food and told me he was leaving. I was terrified. I begged him to let me wake little Peter so we could go with him. But he made me stay. He promised me he would be back as soon as he got enough money to buy our freedom. Then he would take us to some place where we'd be safe. And...and that was the last we ever saw of him."

"Do you think my grandpa might have gone west to the friendly Indians?"

"We have no idea where he went, child," said Ned, "or what happened to him. There were a lot of dangers for Africans in this country. And, still are — mind you, girl. If your grandpa is still alive, he was probably captured somewhere and sold to a plantation down in the south."

"Even if he had managed to get the money somehow and come back ," Bess said in a shaky voice, "we still might not have been freed. The Warrens were so angry. Ned and I wanted to explain, but we doubted they would listen. Right away, they put an advertisement in the newspaper, describing Pompi and offering a reward for their 'runaway' slave."

Ned stood up, working the kinks out of his shoulders. "This old settle is getting mighty uncomfortable, Bess, and the fire's just about died down. I think we should finish the last bit of our talk with Matty tomorrow night."

Chapter Five

"*I* guess that if it wasn't for your papa's doing, all of us might still be slaves."

Bess's words would always stay clear in Matty's memory. She heard them spoken at the beginning of that third and final evening of the family stories.

She recalled sitting with her relatives in front of the fireplace as usual, soaking up a bit of warmth before heading upstairs to their unheated bedrooms. Outside, that particular night, a clear hard coldness had settled over Portsmouth. Now and then, wind swept in off the Piscataqua River to pound against their small house. It rattled loose clapboards, sending icy drafts snaking through cracked plaster walls.

"I have to admit you're right, Bess," said Ned. "We do owe Peter a lot. Sometimes I feel a bit guilty, though, that I didn't take more of a hand in his efforts. But it seemed so uncertain how things would turn out. At times, his behavior got kinda dangerous — for him and for us."

Ned got up from the settle and began poking at the fire with an iron rod. He rearranged several logs to prevent their tumbling out onto the open hearth. Then he picked up Mr. Gray and sat back down, nestling the cat in his arms.

"Right from the beginning, that boy, he was a different kind of fish." Ned shook his head and smiled. "And he was the perfect image of his father."

"A fish? My papa was a fish?" Matty laughed.

"That's just a manner of speaking, child," said Bess. "Peter was always so independent, so sure of himself, almost from the day he came into this world. Didn't take discipline from me hardly at all. Pompi was the one kept a hand on him — when he wasn't spoiling the child. It worried me, though. I was afraid Mrs. Warren might take a dislike to young Peter. Maybe urge her husband to sell him away before she had to deal with another servant who displeased her."

"Oh, that didn't seem too likely to me," said Ned, "not as long as Pompi was here. And Mr. Warren, he seemed almost as pleased with Peter as Pompi was. Took an interest in the child's learning, same as the McIntires did for Bess and me. He liked to teach Peter bits of poems to recite or funny things to say. Then later, he'd get Pompi to bring the child in to perform for visitors."

"I told Pompi that wasn't right," said Bess, "but he couldn't see the harm in it.

Of course all that changed after Pompi went away. Both the Warrens became very strict with us. They wouldn't let us have our extra time off during the week and they kept a close watch on us. Even took away those few books belonging to Pompi and they began burning their newspaper each week so we couldn't read it anymore.

"And, for quite a while, Mr. Warren turned a cold shoulder to Peter. The child didn't understand and I had my hands full trying to keep that six-year-old under control and out of trouble."

Matty was trying to picture how her father must have looked as a child. *Wish someone had painted his portrait,* she thought, *the way they did for Hannah Warren when she was little. But, I don't guess that ever happened for slaves' children.*

Then, a happy idea occurred to her. *I wonder if I could have lessons in painting when we go to our new belong-*

ing place? I could paint portraits of my relatives and hang them in the hallway of our fine house. Later on, folks would know what they looked like.

Ned's voice disrupted Matty's thoughts. "We went through some worrisome years with young Peter, didn't we, Bess. I'll never forget that morning at church when he decided to cause trouble. We might have lost him for sure."

"What did my Papa do?" Matty gave her uncle a worried look.

"Well, he was about your age, Matty, when one awful hot Sunday in August, we were all sitting up in the gallery at church, sweating something terrible. Peter kept fidgeting around and finally, he stands up, right in the middle of the preacher's sermon, and he shouts, 'African people shouldn't have to stay up in this hot gallery': All the white folks down below turned around and glared up at him."

"Thank the good Lord that Ned got him under control," said Bess. "He pulled the child back down on the bench and clamped a hand over his mouth. Then he whispered something in the boy's ear that made him giggle."

"Yes," Ned grinned, "I told him that we was a lot closer to God up there than the white folks was down below."

Matty laughed. Then frowned. "Did Mr. Warren take the whip to Papa when you got home, Gramma?"

"No, child, he didn't. But he did take him into the parlor for a long, angry lecture. And, I heard him threaten to sell Peter away if he didn't behave."

"That threat didn't seem to scare the boy at all," Ned quickly picked up the story. "Not like it always did for us. Of course, after that incident in church, he didn't cause

trouble in public no more, but it was clear he wasn't afraid of
Mr. Warren — or of us, for that matter."

Bess cleared her throat, apparently annoyed at Ned's
interruption. But, he kept on talking.

" As Peter grew older, his work around here started
getting sloppy and he'd duck out of it whenever he could.
Always running off to see the big ships coming in or hanging
around the wharves and the blacksmith's shop, listening to
gossip. I got tired of having to go hunt for him, bring him
home. It's a wonder some kidnapper didn't grab him and sell
him away from here."

"And, the strange thing was," Bess spoke up, shooting
her brother a silencing look, "Mr. Warren didn't seem too
upset about his behavior. I think it was because the man
missed Pompi, their friendship and all, in spite of his leaving.
It wasn't long before Mr. Warren began calling Peter into the
parlor to question the boy about what news he had picked up.
Then I'd hear the same kind of friendly discussions going on
like when Pompi was here."

"Did that get Mrs. Warren all stirred up and mad at
Papa?" Matty was curious as to who would answer. She was
enjoying the storytelling competition between her relatives.

"No," replied Bess, "the woman wasn't paying so much
attention to things by then. She stayed up in her room a lot
of the time. I think it was the outcome of the war that affected
her — that and losing her daughter. Poor Hannah had been
over to France only a few years when she took sick with the
smallpox and soon died.

"You see, the war with England changed things for the
Warrens. They weren't so big in Portsmouth society anymore.

Early in that war, they fell out of favor with folks because Mr. Warren chose the wrong side to be on. He was against the colonies fighting with England and said so publicly. Soon, there were no more grand entertainments in the mansion. And, not many visitors came to the door. Even now, after all these years, I guess some folks in town still haven't forgiven the Warrens for their wartime politics."

"I sure didn't miss all that extra work we used to do," said Ned, "or that gang of their friends and relatives. It was a relief not having to serve those big dinner parties and clean up afterward. We started getting a decent nights' sleep after all that stopped."

"Well, getting back to talking about Peter," Bess heaved an impatient sigh, "he wasn't a bad boy at all. Just restless. And the times were restless, too. Once the war was over, Peter was hearing lots of talk everywhere about the new American nation, how great it was going to be, how everything was going to change for the better.

"In Portsmouth by then — around 1790 or so — more of our people had managed to get their freedom. Quite a few of them had left their masters' houses and were living on their own in town.

"Down in Massachusetts, slavery was finally coming to an end — mostly because some Africans had taken their masters to court and the courts finally declared that slavery was illegal under that state's constitution. Our friends and the officials in the Africans' society, they were saying that slavery would soon be outlawed everywhere in New England."

"Aw, that was just a lot of wasted talk," Ned grumbled. "Nothing really changed for us here in Portsmouth. And, as far as I've heard, the New Hampshire Assembly still hasn't passed a law against owning slaves. And, the nation's government sure isn't stopping it."

"But, Gramma, if other people in town were getting their freedom at that time, why didn't you folks get it, too? Ask Mr. Warren for it?"

"Cause we didn't think it would do any good," Ned spoke up. "And, asking might have caused us grief. You see, I overheard a discussion between the Warrens, one time — him saying that maybe it was time they set us free. But she told him that was nonsense, that we was their lawful property. And, I heard her say that if the law was going to change, then they ought to sell us off quick before it did."

"That was something we'd heard about happening in Portsmouth at that time," said Bess, "...that some slaves were sold off kind of secret like so they wouldn't make a fuss. They were tricked by their masters into going down to the waterfront on errands. Then, when they got there, they were grabbed and sold to sea captains heading south to the plantations."

"Well, you should have just run away in the night like Grandpa Pompi did." Matty was clearly upset by all she had been hearing.

"Oh, Matty!" Ned said in disgust. "Haven't you been listening to what we've been trying to tell you all this time? It was dangerous to make trouble — or try running away. Who knows what would have happened to us. Maybe, looking back, we should have been braver. I don't know. At the time, it just seemed wise to leave things alone, hope for the best.

"And, mind you, girl," he continued, "it is still a dangerous world out there for Africans. Just because you got your freedom document, it won't make you same as white folks. And, it won't keep you safe from some kidnapping slaver, either. You got to be —"

"Ned," Bess interrupted, "let me finish telling her about Peter. Then you can do your lecturing if you want to." She took hold of Matty's hand to reclaim her attention.

"Your papa was not quite sixteen," Bess continued, "when he decided, without saying anything to us, to take matters into his own hands. One morning, he marched right into Mr. Warren's parlor and boldly told him he wanted his freedom. There was a dreadful, loud argument and I was shaking with fear. I stepped into the pantry so I wouldn't have to hear it.

"But, do you know, child… after a while, things quieted down in the parlor and a short time later, Peter came walking back into the kitchen, all smiles. He informed Ned and me that Mr. Warren said he would give all of us our freedom, but only after Peter learned a proper trade. He said he wanted the boy to be able to earn a living.

"A few days later, Peter was sent to learn blacksmithing at the shop back of here on Bow Street. It was the best thing for him. Never saw the boy so happy. Turned out, he had a real talent for putting bits of iron together in clever ways.

"After about a year or so, Peter learned enough to start getting a small wage, but the blacksmith always paid the money to Mr. Warren. When the boy argued about that, Mr. Warren promised Peter that he would give him half of everything he earned when the time came for us to be freed. Exactly when that would be, he didn't say."

"That was a mean cat and mouse game he was playing

with us," Ned spoke up.

"Anyway," said Bess, "when Peter was just nineteen, he met your future mama. You should have seen what a happy, good looking couple they made.

"Peter was determined to marry Matilda right away, but there was a problem. She was the daughter of free Africans and Mrs. Warren didn't want her living with us because she might be too independent and cause trouble. Mrs. Warren tried to stop her husband from giving permission for the marriage, but I guess he figured Peter would just run off if he didn't."

"And, then," Ned reached over and tickled Matty, " a year and a half later, this little bundle of sunshine arrived."

"Gramma?"

"What, child?"

Matty hesitated, then asked, "How long did my mama live after I came?"

"Only a few weeks," Bess sighed. "My heart ached for your papa. He was such a lost soul after Matilda died. Stopped caring about his work or getting free to start a new life or anything. He left your care mostly up to me and Ned. It took an awful long time for him to get his courage back.

"It wasn't until you were nearly five years old that he did. One night, after you were put to bed, Peter sat down with us and told us he had waited long enough. He was going to talk with Mr. Warren the next morning and if the man still refused to give us our freedom, Peter said he would just take you and quietly go away."

"I tried to talk him out of that, the going away," said Ned, "but he told me not to worry. He said he'd heard about places in the middle of some big cities like Philadelphia and Boston where lots of Africans were living in freedom and there was wasn't much fear of being kidnapped and sold back into slavery."

"And then, Matty," said Bess, "well, you know what happened after that — Mr. Warren finally agreeing to free us and our trip up to the town clerk's office and all. Your papa insisted our freedom documents had to have all the official signatures so we would be protected under the law."

"Do you think Papa went to one of those big cities, that maybe he got sick or something there and can't get back to us? Or send us a letter?"

"We don't know, child." Bess put her arm around Matty, drawing her closer. "And, maybe we never will. I know how hard it's been for you, waiting all this time for him, believing he'll come back, especially at this time of year. And, I'm not saying he never will, but—"

"You think he's dead, don't you!" Matty angrily pulled away and stood up to face her relatives. "That's what all this storytelling's been about. Well, I don't! He's alive. I know it. It's too soon to stop hoping."

Before anyone could reply, Matty rushed up the stairs, tears nearly blinding her.

She paid no attention when Bess called her to come back down for Bible reading and prayers.

Chapter Six
24 December 1806

"*M*atty? I won't call you again! You get your body out of that bed this minute. You hear me?"

"Yes Gramma." Matty yanked the covers up over her head, causing Gray cat to yowl as he leaped down onto the floor.

"You know it's baking day…and, there's a ton of work ahead of us," Bess called up the steps. "Mr. Warren wants the mansion in proper order for Christmas visitors this evening."

For a moment or two, all was silent, upstairs and down.

"Do I have to come up there for you?"

"No, Gramma. I'm coming."

"See that you do. I've left the water buckets for you by the pantry door. And don't dawdle. Mrs. Warren's breakfast tray will be ready soon."

Matty listened as Bess's heavy footsteps took her out of their house and on into the mansion.

"Mr. Warren wants, Mr. Warren wants," she mimicked, "I'm tired of 'Mr. Warren wants'. When is it going to be 'Matty wants' ?"

She fished under the covers for her wool socks which had come off during the night. Pulling them on, she stepped out onto the cold floor of the chilly room. She grabbed yesterday's clothes off their wall pegs, hopped back into bed and threw the covers over her head. Under her makeshift tent she took off her nightgown and proceeded to get dressed. It was a tangled kind of effort, putting on two petticoats and a work dress under there, but she preferred that to the teeth chattering alternative.

And all the while, her young mind was struggling with those worry-loaded words so casually spoken by Bess — Christmas visitors.

"The only visitor I want to hear about is Papa," she said. But, inside her head, another voice, came forth to argue. Silly girl, it chided, it's time you stopped your foolish hoping. You might as well face it. He's never coming back.

"No," Matty said. "I won't believe that. Oh, I wish I could stay in bed and sleep right on through this Christmas. Then I wouldn't have to keep wondering if he's coming — or not. Or, keep thinking about all that worrisome stuff from Gramma's stories."

Throwing back the bedcovers, Matty stepped into her rundown work shoes and went over to an old chest of drawers to get a clean dust cap. At that predawn hour, only the stingiest bit of light from a small window allowed her to glance around the crowded room. Besides her bed and Bess's larger one, there was just enough space for a night stand with its washbasin and chamber pot, and that chest, a battered, legless mansion castoff now squatting inelegantly on wooden blocks. Other than a small looking glass over the chest, the walls were bare of decoration, perhaps a result of Bess's no-nonsense attitude.

Matty scowled at the face in the looking glass while she forced her unruly mass of short curly black hair under the ruffled cap. She grinned, then stuck her tongue out at her reflection. Throwing a woolen shawl around her shoulders, she headed down stairs to the first floor, entered the pantry and quietly closed the door. At the other end of the narrow room, beyond the closed mansion kitchen door, she heard Bess's commanding voice and Ned's short replies.

Instead of picking up the water buckets and going on outside, she lingered in the well-stocked pantry to enjoy its mouthwatering odors. Smoked hams and sausage, cloth-wrapped cheeses, strings of dried apples and pumpkin bits — all touched her nose and made her stomach rumble with hunger. From among the many covered crocks of preserved foods on the shelves came the spicy aroma of mincemeat, Matty's favorite. She was sorely tempted to slide her fingers beneath that crock's lid for a sticky sample, but feared getting caught.

Instead, she fished around beneath the straw in a large barrel, drew out two bright green apples and put them in her apron pocket. Opening the back door, Matty stepped out into a quiet world, one deeply covered by fresh snow.

Following along Ned's shoveled path, Matty soon reached the well in the back yard. She lowered the first bucket on a rope pulley and hauled it up again, straining at the effort of lifting it up and over the well's high boxed rim. Once the second bucket was lowered, she paused to stamp her feet while looking around. Playfully, she puffed clouds of white vapor into the cold air.

Kind of smoky this morning, she thought. Hope the wind comes up to drive it away before the rest of the town wakes up and gets their fires going. Matty hated those days when a haze of acrid smoke, belching forth from hundreds of chimneys, settled down over the town.

At that early hour, only a few snow-muffled sounds reached her ears. Somewhere beyond the high board fence separating the mansion's narrow back yard from the rest of the crowded neighborhood, several dogs were barking. Overhead, a noisy seagull also broke the stillness. Nearer at hand, in the carriage barn, Matty heard a snorting and stomping of hooves. She smiled at the thought of old Dobbin calling to her or perhaps just greeting the spotted cow in the stall next to his.

Which, of course, reminded her of the reason for one of the apples in her pocket. Ignoring the second bucket still down in the well, Matty headed toward the animals and their cozy warmth.

"Such a good old fella," she said to Dobbin, as she rubbed the horse's forehead and planted a kiss on his velvety muzzle. Palming an apple, she offered it for his enjoyment. "Wish I could stay here and have one of our talks. Or, better yet," she suddenly thought, "I'd like to climb on your back right now and we'd just gallop away from here. And, we'd never come back. "

"Matty? Where are you?" Ned called out from the back door. "What's taking you so long? Your gramma's getting cross. She wants you in the house, now."

"I'm coming, Uncle." Matty returned to the well and hauled up the neglected bucket. Grasping the wet, cold rope handle of each bucket, she cautiously small-stepped along the slippery path back to the house.

"I shouldn't have to do all this hard work," she mumbled. "I got my freedom document. I'm not a slave anymore. If Papa can't come for me, maybe I ought to go find a safe belonging place, myself."

⊷ ≖≼✦≽≖ ⊶

A blast of hot, smoky air greeted Matty as she entered the mansion kitchen. She emptied her buckets into the water barrel, replaced its lid and turned to watch the goings on at the fireplace. Ned was tending to a fire blazing away inside the brick bake oven which was located at the back of the large walk-in recess.

Baking day, Matty thought. Just more hard work. She watched while bursts of flame shot out of the oven's fiery mouth and licked their way on up the huge open chimney. Below the oven, to the right, a log fire was also roaring away, creating lots of hot coals for Bess's ongoing cooking operations. In a few hours, once the inside dome of the oven was heated and the fire there died down, Matty knew it would be her task to sweep it clean of ashes so baking could begin.

"Don't just stand there daydreaming," Bess called out from her work table, her command post. "Take Mrs. Warren's breakfast tray up-stairs before everything gets cold."

Matty avoided making eye-contact with her grand-mother. She approached the table, carefully lifted the round silver tray with it's cloth-covered dishes and walked out into the shadowy back hallway. Ned closed the door behind her.

On the stair landing above, the clock loudly struck the hour of six as Matty ignored the entrance to the servants' staircase and headed up the grand one, instead.

"Good morning, friends," she whispered to her beloved Indian kings.

Upon reaching the second floor hallway, she gently tapped at Mrs Warren's door and then opened it. Stepping cautiously through the cold, darkened, musty-smelling room, Matty set the tray down on a large tea table near the fireplace. She removed the fire screen and coaxed a bit of flame from the pile of still hot ashes before adding small kindling wood. Despite the immediate heat, it would be a long while before its warmth penetrated even half of that large, high ceiling room. As Matty proceeded to open the shutters on the windows, behind her she heard the soft rustle of silk bed hangings. Old Mrs Warren was slowly emerging from the shrouded enclosure.

"Good morning, Missus," Matty said, knowing there would be no answer. She had never heard the woman speak or show any sign of interest in anyone. Sometimes, she did reach out a frail hand to Mr. Gray when he came to visit, but that was all. Matty helped her put on a quilted robe and then settled her in a chair by the table.

Normally, the girl would have stayed long enough to make the bed and take away the covered chamber pot, but this morning the bright dawning light from a tall east window caught her attention. Hastily, she replaced the fire screen.

"Excuse me, Missus," she said, "I'll be right back."

Knowing that she shouldn't, Matty quickly left the room, scampered up the back stairway and on up the winding steps into the rooftop cupola. After yesterday's disappointing, snow-blocked view, Matty was eager to watch the sun coming up over Portsmouth.

And, it promised to be quite a show. Beneath a bank of low, thinly scattered clouds, the sun's early rays streamed up the river and over the town, casting a pinkish orange glow on windows and snow-covered roofs. Matty circled around in the tiny room enjoying the sights. Her eyes traveled west up Daniel Street to the Square, then southward over snow-clogged streets and alleyways toward Puddle Dock and the town of New Castle, far beyond. Finally, she turned to gaze northward past the river and then on up Bow Street to Chapel hill and then, — she stopped. In horror!

"NO! No, no!" she screamed. Her frantic cries of 'fire...fire' echoed through the old mansion as she plunged down the cupola steps and rushed on down to the first floor.

"There's a terrible big fire down at Bow Street corner," she shouted, bursting into Mr. Warren's parlor and slamming the door against the wall.

"Hush your noise girl," Bess called out as she and Ned hurried toward her.

Outside, steeple bells everywhere began clanging in steady, counted intervals in order to alert the citizenry. Over the din and excitement, old Mr. Warren sat up straighter on his daybed and began issuing orders. He didn't look well at all.

"Ned, you go on up the hill to see what's happening," he said. "Take our fire buckets with you and leave them with the men, but get back here as quick as you can.

"Bess, if that fire should come our way, we'll need to get ready to abandon this house.

"Matty, girl," Warren continued, "you get back up in that cupola and keep watch."

"Oh, I couldn't do that, Mister. I'm...I'm scared! We need to leave town now!" She backed away in fear.

"Nonsense," said the man. "We'll stay right here until we know how big that fire is and if it might be coming our way. You must keep watch for any fires that might start up elsewhere in town."

"But I didn't make Mrs. Warren's bed and her chamber pot is still —"

"Never mind that," Bess interrupted. "Don't you sass Mr. Warren. You do as you're told. And, take a blanket off a bed so you can bundle up while you're in that cupola."

Reluctantly, Matty climbed the grand staircase. Below her, she heard Mr. Warren saying, "I pray this fire isn't going to be a big one, Bess. We don't need another disaster like that one four years ago at Christmas time."

— ⛌ ⛌ —

Up in the cupola, a frightened Matty kept nervously pacing back and forth, dutifully looking among hundreds of smoking house chimneys for any signs of unusual smoke or fire. But, other than the ones now raging on Bow Street near the corner of Market, there were none. Despite being bundled in a shawl and blanket, she couldn't stop shivering. "I don't want to be here. I don't want to be here," she kept repeating.

Matty's greatest terror was fire. It had been ever since that awful one on the day after Christmas in 1802. Now, as she stared down at the billowing clouds of smoke and shooting flames at Bow corner, memories flooded forth. She saw herself as she was back then, a tearful five-year-old, huddled in a corner by the open front door of the mansion, clutching her rag doll. The whole place was in an uproar that morning. Bess and Ned kept rushing back and forth, piling furniture, trunks, books, food and other stuff into a horse-drawn wagon waiting out front. Matty watched Mr. Warren cut Hannah's portrait out of its frame. Then he rolled it up and told Ned to take it away with other rolled up portraits.

From a block or so away, toward Market Square, little Matty heard shouting and frightening noises as people fought the fires. And, the terrifying smell of smoke was drifting ever closer to the mansion's open door.

"Don't you dare move from there until I tell you to," was Bess's stern warning when she first sat Matty by the door. But, as people and bundles kept passing her by, the child's fear and impatience grew.

"Please let me get into the wagon," she called out several times.

"Not now," came the only reply.

Finally, Matty heard Mr. Warren tell Ned to drive the wagon out to his farm in Newington, up river from Portsmouth. Without waiting for permission, the frightened child scooted out the door and crawled into the loaded wagon. Burrowing in under an overturned chair, she pulled soft bundles around her.

"You didn't mind me, girl," Bess scolded when she and her brother finally climbed up onto the driver's seat. "You gotta learn to do what I tell you."

Taking up the reins, Ned gently encouraged a nervous Dobbin to turn left, down Rosemary Lane and then, within a block or so, turn right onto Buck Street. They needed to find a safe route out around the burning center of town. Occasionally, as the wagon rumbled along, Matty peeked out, only to burrow down again, terrified at the flaming sights.

After going west for several blocks, Ned located a cross street that was free of flames. Turning the wagon north, they gratefully headed for the safety of the farm four miles away.

Only much later did Matty learn the full details of that dreadful day. A pre-dawn fire started just south of Market Square and swiftly spread north to buildings along both sides of Market Street and on down toward Bow. Aided by strong winds, the fires soon turned the corner down Daniel Street. Rapidly, on either side of the street, whole blocks of tightly-packed wooden buildings burst into flames. Families and shopkeepers frantically threw what possessions they could save out into the streets while bucket brigades bravely tried to quench the fires. But it was hopeless. No matter how quickly the line of volunteers threw buckets of water onto the fires or poured water into the pumper tubs, there was no stopping the flames. Feeble streams from small, short hoses on the water pumpers were all but useless.

In a desperate attempt to stop the fires from spreading, men began pulling down some unburned buildings directly in its paths. While men with axes cut into a building's corner posts, teams of other men threw large

curved hooks attached to ropes onto the roof to begin pulling it apart. Then they would attack the side walls.

By the time the wind finally died down that day and the fires burned out, Portsmouth had lost a great many buildings. Dozens of families were homeless. As fate would have it, though, the fires stopped just a block or so from the Warren mansion.

⸻

A sound of heavy footsteps on the cupola stairs brought Matty's thoughts back to the present.

"This should ease your hunger, child," said Bess, as her head and shoulders appeared over the top of the stairwell. She handed Matty a mug of cider and a tin plate containing a thick slice of buttered toast and a fat sausage.

"Whew! Those stairs are steep," Bess huffed, as she cleared the top step. From just behind her, Mr. Gray streaked through the opening and sprang onto the circular bench. Eying the food, he purred loudly as Matty sat down beside him.

Bess took a moment to look out the windows toward the fires. " Doesn't seem right that fires should comes to us on such a clear, beautiful day. Anyway, just so you know, Ned told Mr. Warren that he thinks those fires probably won't be as bad as that last time. There's no wind at all to drive them. Ned says the corner fish market and two ships tied up back of there are destroyed, but the fire brigades are working fast to get things under control."

"Then I don't need to stay up here," Matty mumbled over a mouthful of food.

"Indeed you do," Bess replied. "Mr. Warren needs a good lookout. He suspects we may have a firebug in this town. No telling what may happen."

"But what if the wind does come up…and the fires start spreading our way?"

"Then we'll all leave town like we did before. There's no need to worry."

"Gramma," Matty reached out and took Bess's hand. "Couldn't we just leave here now? Go away to Boston? We'd be safe if we all stayed together and we could try finding Papa and —"

"Matty, you stop such talk right now," Bess cut in. "I won't hear of such an idea. Running away is foolish. Always has been. Can't you get that through your head after all we've been telling you?"

"But, Gramma, what if Mr. Warren should die? What will happen to us, then?"

"He's not dying. And, anyway, he said he's planning to provide for us in his will if we stay on and see him and Mrs. Warren out to the burial ground."

"If… if Papa comes back before then, will we leave?"

"Now, look here, Matty! You got to get your mind away from all that. We can't keep going round and round on the same old tread mill. Your Uncle Ned and I explained about our situation here. You've got to learn to be content with how things are.

"You just stay up here and mind Mr. Warren's instructions. I must get back to my work." With that said, Bess eased her stout self back down the cupola steps.

From below, Matty heard the clock strike nine. Sharing the last bit of her sausage with Mr. Gray, she gathered him into her arms, nestling him in part of her blanket. From her vantage point, she quickly assured herself there were no fires starting up elsewhere in town. Then she resumed gazing at the on-going fires. It was a haunting sight, those piles of blackened timbers where businesses and rooming houses once stood. Lower Bow Street was littered with people's furniture and other possessions. Half way up the hill, off to one side, she noticed an old sofa crowded with small children. Several women huddled near by. Matty shivered at the thought of their discomfort and fear.

She did notice little wisps of smoke beginning to drift out of several other buildings further up Bow hill next to the river. But she saw no flames. Remembering what Uncle Ned had reported about the lack of any wind, Matty decided there was no need for alarm. The brigades will see to it all, she told herself. Suddenly remembering the other apple in her pocket, she withdrew it and began munching away.

In her mind the turmoil over her own situation began competing with the turmoil beyond the windows. She got to thinking about what she said aloud that morning on her way back from the well. She had surprised herself in giving voice to the dangerous idea of going off alone to find a belonging place. But now she gave that idea more thought.

"I bet I could do it," she whispered. "I could hide in the woods during the day and travel only at night. And, I'd take lots of cheese and bread to keep from getting hungry. I'm not scared of kidnapping slavers. They wouldn't find me, no sir.

"Once I got to Boston, I'd go looking for Papa; maybe ask some kind African family to help me. Then, I'd tell them —"

BAM! BOOM! A series of loud explosions rattled the cupola windows and shook the old mansion. Jumping up, Matty saw flames shooting out of a warehouse near the top of Bow hill, just across from St. John's Church. Flaming debris had landed on the roof of the old church and was rapidly igniting the wooden shingles. And, adding to Matty's horror was the realization that the church was only three buildings away from the Warren mansion.

As before, she rushed pell-mell down the stairs to alert people below.

Chapter Seven

"*O*h, the church! Not the church! How awful!"

A chorus of frightened voices surrounded a shivering Matty as she stood out in the middle of Chapel Street. Above her, up on the hill, ugly clouds of black smoke were billowing into the bright blue sky. Bess was calling to her from the back yard, but Matty ignored her. She couldn't move or take her eyes from the terrible scene.

Despite the covering of snow on the church roof, the flaming debris from the explosion was quickly eating into its wooden shingles as well as those which covered the upper part of the tall steeple. Somewhere down below, a brave soul was desperately ringing the steeple bell to alert the town.

"Out of our way, girl," shouted several men behind Matty as they rushed up the street with fire buckets, ladders and axes. Behind them came a horse-drawn sleigh carrying two water pumpers. The wild-eyed team kept slipping and sliding on the snowy hill. Now and then, Matty saw sparks fly when their iron-shod hooves struck stones beneath the snow.

"Matty, get back in the house," called Ned, as he ran down the hill toward her. "No, don't stop me with questions." He grabbed her arm and, not too gently, hurried her into the house. Without stopping, he rushed on through the mansion to the parlor. Bess and Matty quickly followed.

"It was the rum barrels, Mr. Warren, hundreds of them. They up and blew the warehouse apart. Sent burning timbers onto the church roof and onto some other roofs by the waterfront." Ned paused to catch his breath.

Matty was suddenly struck by how old her uncle looked. His dark brown face had a grayish tinge and he appeared more tired than she'd ever seen him. She wanted to push a chair toward him, but she knew he would never sit down in Mr. Warren's presence. None of them ever did.

"Most of the burning stuff flew north, out over the river," Ned continued," but there's a bit of wind coming up now and there's no telling which direction it'll settle on. Some of the fire fighters are already starting to tear apart the unburned parsonage next door to the church. Others are taking axes to a couple of houses further down towards us. That should stop the flames' spreading — unless the wind gets going."

"Dreadful...just dreadful," said Mr. Warren. "And, we just finished building that new parsonage, too." Nervously, he ran his fingers through his gray hair and shook his head. "But I am glad the men are doing what's needed."

Turning from his desk where he had been bundling up business papers, he asked,

"Bess, how far along are you with preparations for leaving?"

"Ned's got all the silver goods packed up and he's been getting clothes and things down from upstairs." Bess looked and sounded even more exhausted than her brother. "And I've started packing up the pantry foods. The oven's just about ready for putting the pies in, but I guess there won't be time for that. I was on my way upstairs to get Mrs. Warren dressed when those explosions hit."

"I put sled runners on the wagon," said Ned, "and Dobbin's hitched to it so I can bring him around front whenever you say to."

And, I've been doing my part, Matty was tempted to add, but she guessed nobody cared to ask about that.

"Well," said Mr. Warren, "everybody keep on with the work as quickly as you can. I just hope we won't need to leave this time."

Later on, as the clock struck half past two, Matty slumped down on a pile of rolled bedding in the cold front hallway, grateful for a rest. She'd never had to work so hard and so steadily before. Her grandmother was seated on a lower step of the grand staircase, rubbing at tired, swollen ankles. Most every space in the hallway was filled with a jumble of the Warrens' furniture — at least what was most portable — as well as bundles and baskets of house-hold valuables.

"Gramma, are we going to leave or not? It's still smelling awful smoky out there."

"Just keep your voice down, Matty. Ned's on good watch out in the street. He'll let us know if any fires are starting up again."

Behind the closed west parlor door, both the elderly Warrens sat waiting, fully dressed for travel, including hats and gloves. For Matty and Bess, it had been an exhausting struggle getting a confused and frightened Mrs. Warren into proper clothing and forcing her to leave the bedchamber. They all but carried the woman down the stairs.

"My goodness," Bess suddenly spoke up. "Just look at that fool cat. He'll break his neck one of these days."

Near the front door, Mr. Gray had climbed up over piled furniture and was doing a balancing act in among the sharp prongs of a set of caribou horns mounted on the wall.

"Oh, he's all right," said Matty, "I've seen him up there lots of times...and he makes a good duster, too." Matty shifted about, trying to get comfortable.

"Gramma, when are we going to eat? I'm so hungry I could chew on a skunk!"

"Won't hurt us to miss a meal now and then," Bess replied. She studied her granddaughter's face for a moment. "It's been a difficult day for you, child. I know that and I'm so sorry you have to go through all this frightful business again. But then, maybe you don't remember much about that other fire in 1802. You were so little then."

"Oh, I remember!" was Matty's quick, short reply.

Bess kept looking intently at her until Matty lowered her eyes. She had the uncomfortable feeling that her grandmother might be trying to read her thoughts. *I'd be in real trouble if she could. Gramma would tan my hide for even thinking about running off. But what else can I do? I don't want to be stuck here forever.*

Earlier, during that brief time when she had been standing out in the street watching the fires, Matty made up her mind. *If Papa doesn't come for me this Christmas, it'll be up to me to find that safe belonging place for us. And, I better do it soon.*

"Come on, child." Bess broke the silence and stood up. "We still need to pack up our clothes and things. I just hope there'll be room for them in that wagon after the Warrens' things are all packed. And, girl, you get that worried look off your face. We will all be safe in the end."

Not in a town that keeps burning down, Matty wanted to shout. And, not when kidnapping slavers might still get us.

Following behind her grandmother, all the girl could think about was leaving. Alone. Suddenly a thought struck her. I can't leave without my freedom document. I wonder where Gramma's keeping it?

"I've got good news, Bess," Ned called out as he hurried in through the pantry, slamming the door behind him. "We don't have to leave. They've stopped the fires from spreading and most of the big ones are just about out. And, praise the Lord, the wind has gone still."

"What about the church?" asked Bess, helping Ned off with his overcoat.

"There's nothing left of it. Just a sea of ashes."

Ned hardly finished speaking when the pantry door flew open and a group of white men stormed in. Their faces and clothing were streaked with soot and they were laughing and talking to one another. Ignoring the servant family, they carelessly stomped snow and mud across Bess's clean kitchen floor and headed on through the mansion in search of Mr. Warren.

Curious as what was going on, Matty and her family quietly followed them and stopped just outside the open parlor door to listen. In the noisy scene that followed, the men all talked at once, eagerly telling details of the fires, what was lost and what was done to bring them under control. Mr. Warren kept asking questions and it was obvious he was enjoying all the excitement and attention.

Beside him, Mrs. Warren still sat, doll-like in her fancy clothes. She hadn't moved from the stiff-backed chair where Bess and Matty had placed her hours ago. Matty felt sad at seeing the old woman's blank, joyless face.

Suddenly, Joshua Warren looked toward the doorway and his servants standing there. "Isn't this just the best news," he called to them. "Once again, this house has been spared the ravage of flames.

"Now, then, Bess," he continued, "we must find something to feed these brave fellows. We will have a celebration! By golly, this is going to be a happy Christmas after all! And, that reminds me," he went on talking to his servants. "I want to give each of you your Christmas presents right now." He reached into his waistcoat pocket and took out some small coins.

Following his nodded invitation, Bess and then Ned each came forward to receive a silver half dime. After saying a quiet "thank you, Sir" the elderly twins left the room, heading for the kitchen. Matty noticed that neither of them was smiling and she felt a sudden burning resentment. In Warren's excitement, he had thoughtlessly heaped more work on the tired shoulders of his sixty-year old servants. After their long, exhausting day, they were now expected to summon the strength to restore order to the mansion — at least in the downstairs area — while preparing for this spur-of-the-moment celebration.

Matty still lingered by the parlor doorway. The idea of a gift usually lit up her face, but not this time. She stepped forward, unsmiling, to receive Mr. Warren's offered coin.

"Now here is a fine girl," said Mr. Warren, addressing the men around him. "This youngster was a brave little lookout. She kept a good watch up in our cupola."

The men all laughed, making Matty feel uncomfortable and foolish, somehow. She grabbed the half dime and fled from the room, forgetting to say thank you. Behind her, she heard more laughter and some rude comments about her.

Anger surged forth at Mr. Warren and the others. He doesn't care at all about us, she thought, expecting us to keep working so hard with no time for food and rest. He still treats us like we were his slaves. And we're not! No, not anymore!

"Matty," called Bess, "come along and stop your dawdling." She and Ned stood beside her work table, making plans. Bess instructed her brother, "After you've gotten Dobbin unhitched and fed, you best get a fire going in the other parlor. We'll put the supper table in there. And, you'll need a good supply of fresh candles for both parlors and the hallway, of course. And, Matty, you get going on peeling potatoes 'til Ned gets back. Then you and he can start clearing out the hallway."

Saying nothing, Matty did as she was told. Now and then, as she worked, she reached into her apron pocket to finger the silver coin — her first, ever. That should come in real handy, she told herself, when I make my trip to Boston.

U.S. half dime

Chapter Eight

*D*arkness had set in by the time Ned and Matty finished clearing the front hallway of furniture and bundles. Some things they carried back up stairs. The rest were put in a small room off the back hallway until after the supper was served.

During most of the time they were working, Matty kept silent, her mind elsewhere. And it was clear Ned found her behavior strange. He obviously missed her chatterbox ways because he kept trying to get her talking or make her laugh. In a effort to lighten her mood, he joked, "this sure is a mighty peculiar way to celebrate the Christmas, moving furniture back and forth."

"I guess." Matty gave him a half-hearted smile.

Ned tried again. "Well, cheer up, girl. Tomorrow morning I'm sure you'll have a much bigger smile on your face when you open your presents."

No doubt, he was thinking of the little writing box with Matty's name carved on it which he'd secretly been making and also of the pretty blue, hooded cloak that Bess had been sewing on out of Matty's sight.

I wish I could talk to Uncle Ned, Matty thought, tell him about my plans.

It's so lonely keeping it all to myself. But he'd surely talk me out of it or maybe tell Gramma. I just better keep quiet so I don't let something slip out.

More than once, as they worked together, Matty's tears welled up and she choked them back. She kept her head down so Ned wouldn't notice. Silently, she continued going over possible plans and reassuring herself. I can do it, she thought. I know I can. I just got to be brave like Papa told me.

She and Ned were getting ready to move a large dining table from the back hallway into the east parlor when there came a loud knocking at the front door. Leaving Matty at the far end of the table, Ned took up a lantern and went to open the door. For a brief moment, all was quiet. Then Matty heard her uncle exclaim, "Oh, my Lord! Oh, my!"

In the dim light, Matty saw a tall, well-dressed African man enter the hall. He hugged Ned and then came toward her. She couldn't move or speak. She felt like a stone.

Was it him? Was it really him? She burst into tears as her father quickly gathered her into his arms. Without saying a word, he carried her down the hallway in search of Bess.

⋯ ⚎ ⋯

This time, a noisy, happy scene took place in the kitchen instead of in the parlor. Bess and Matty, were weeping with joy as well as relief. Ned tried to hide his tears, but soon gave up. It was so wonderful to know that Peter was alive and safe. All work was forgotten while everyone, except Matty, rapidly talked and questioned Peter.

"Where were you? What happened? Why didn't you write to us? What kept you away so long?"

For Matty, there was only one question she wanted to ask, only one thing she needed to know. While she waited for a pause in the excitement, she tucked herself under part of her father's long woolen cloak, leaned in against the stool where he sat and hung onto his arm.

Peter's rapid replies and the swirl of grown-up conversation

overwhelmed Matty's mind. She took in only stray bits and pieces — something about pirates capturing the ship her father was on and his being forced to join their crew, then the pirate ship being seized by a British man-of-war and her father taken to a London prison. And, something about his freedom paper enabling him to get released.

"I'm sure glad I still had that document," Matty heard her father say.

"But what took you so long in getting back?" asked Bess.

"I had to get work and save enough money for passage home," Peter replied. "And, I had lot of problems doing that."

"Well, you could have at least sent us a letter to ease our worrying," Bess said crossly.

"I did send one, Momma. But I guess it got lost or maybe went down with a ship. Pirates of one country or another are everywhere on the high seas. I'm lucky I even got back here."

At last, Matty threw off the cloak and reached up to take her father's face in both her hands. She looked him straight in the eyes. "Papa, did you...did you find a safe place for us...a place where we can belong?"

"I surely did," Peter replied with a grin. I've rented part of a house in Boston, near the waterfront where I work."

"What kind of work did you find," asked Ned.

"Uncle, I've really had some luck. I've got a good-paying job in a blacksmith's shop. And, the owner – an elderly black man – says he might sell the business to me in a year or so. And Matty," Peter continued, "you will be happy to know that we'll be living in a wonderful neighborhood with other free African families and there's lots of children for you to play with. And, there's even a school for you to go to.

"And," said Peter, looking across the work table at his

mother, "there's plenty of room in my part of the Boston house for you and Uncle Ned."

"Oh no," Bess shook her head. "We're much too old to be going anywhere. And besides, the Warrens still need us and —"

"Bess! You listen here," Ned interrupted her. "We're not too old. And why should we stay here, working so hard? When the Warrens do pass away — and that time is likely not far off — where will we go then? I can't believe he's planning to leave us enough money to live on."

Everyone waited while Bess looked around at her family, first one face and then the next. Then, to everyone's delight, she laughed and slapped the table. "By Heaven, you're right, Brother Ned. We will go to Boston with Peter and Matty."

Their happiness was suddenly interrupted when the hallway door to the kitchen was slammed open by one of Mr. Warren's visitors. "You there, boy," he pointed at Ned, "your master wants to see you. Now!" The man turned and stomped back toward the parlor.

Peter reached out and put a gentle hand on his uncle's shoulder. "Never mind, Uncle Ned. You stay here. I'll attend to this."

Matty was not about to let her father out of her sight. Quickly, she followed after him, grabbing onto his hand as they walked out of the kitchen.

Without knocking, Peter opened the west parlor door and stepped inside. Matty stayed close beside him.

"Good evening, Mr. Warren. Good evening, Mrs. Warren," he said politely.

Joshua Warren made no reply. He, like the rest of his company, simply stared in astonishment at the well-dressed, dignified young African in their midst.

"Sir," Peter spoke calmly, "I have come to tell you that my family will no longer serve in this household. Now that I have found work and a place for us in Boston, we will all be leaving Portsmouth in a few days."

To Matty's surprise, still no one made a sound as her father continued.

"If you wish, Mr. Warren, we can stay on here until then and help you get your house back in order. Now, I will go back to my family in the kitchen and await your reply."

With that said, Peter led his daughter out of the parlor and quietly closed the door. A flurry of loud conversation erupted in the room behind them, but they paid no attention.

Half way down the hallway, Matty tugged hard on her father's arm, slowing their progress. Peter stopped and knelt down beside her. Above their heads were the fire buckets, now hanging back in place. And, just above there was an empty iron hook and a faint circular stain where a threatening leather whip once hung.

"Papa, I 'm so glad you came back," said Matty, putting her head on his shoulder. "Sometimes it was so hard for me to keep believing and…and I almost…" Matty stopped, not wanting to tell him more. Instead, she changed the subject. "Papa, do you have enough money to buy me a pretty new dress…before we go to Boston?"

Peter laughed and hugged her. "Of course I do, Little One. And, when we get to Boston, we'll buy lots more, lots of new things for you and the family. It's going to be such a good life for us there, you'll see."

Epilogue
BOSTON, MASSACHUSETTS
23 December 1863

I wish that all the stories of my life had ended so happily. That's not to say I've had an unhappy life since we left Portsmouth. Things just didn't all turn out quite the way I'd hoped for. Over the years, like most folks, we've had our share of Fortune's frowns as well as her smiles.

At first, though, our move to Boston was wonderful. There was everything here that Papa promised and more. His business did well for a while, though we never became wealthy the way he and I hoped we would.

I remember being thrilled at having lots of playmates close by and going to school with other African children. And, on Sundays when we attended the African Baptist Church at the new meeting house, we sat in comfortable pews on the *first* floor, surrounded by welcoming, friendly people. I came to understand more fully what Papa meant about belonging and having the freedom to choose one's place in the world.

Gramma and Great Uncle Ned were delighted with their new surroundings. I marveled at how much happier, even younger, they looked. Gramma still made me do lots of housework, but she wasn't so stern about it. Wasn't long before I started taking pleasure in it because it was done for my family. My childhood worries and nightmares about kidnapping slavers soon faded away.

One morning, a week or so after we arrived in town, Papa proudly announced that I had a new last name — Smith. (He chose it because of his blacksmith business.) He told us we needed to put reminders of slavery behind us. But Gramma Bess said she'd just as soon keep the Warren part and that I ought to keep it in case there would ever be a legal problem regarding the name on our freedom documents. Uncle Ned said he didn't much care one way or the other.

In later years, after I married James Johnson, I could boast of three last names. My daughters, Wila and Ann, though, they think I ought to stop using that slave name. Maybe they're right. Sometimes, though, its hard to cast off something that's been a part of you so long, even if it does have an unpleasant connection.

That tenement house which Papa brought us to, the one we shared with three other families, it wasn't the big mansion I dreamed of, but it was pleasant and I loved the view from our third floor rooms — and I still do — almost like my glorious cupola. Thanks to Papa's hard work, we own this building now. Someday I must write Papa's story in more detail, about his sea-going adventures with those pirates and about his many years of dedicated work in the African Society and in their efforts to end slavery.

As for my accomplishments in life, I was a good student and later on I was hired as a school teacher in our neighborhood. It was such joy being with children everyday, watching their bright minds soar. As for my ambition of becoming an artist and painting portraits of my family, try as I did, I just never had the talent for it. Thank goodness there's a new invention now that makes pictures of us, if we have the money.

I don't think I can keep writing any more, today. My elderly fingers are getting numb and it's hard to hold the pen. And, that fool cat, Marble, keeps reaching a paw towards the inkwell. Guess he wants his supper.

Also, my mind keeps shifting away from young Matty's happiness. Thoughts of later years intrude — Fortune's frowns. Though our Boston neighborhood was a haven for us, it wasn't long before I learned of the world beyond and came face to face with some of the painful realities for Africans in this country. Down through the years, Uncle Ned's words of caution often echoed in my head. He was so right. My freedom document was just a beginning.

I think that, even if the Union Army does win this war and slavery is finally ended everywhere in the country, we still may have a long way to go before there is real freedom and respect among the races.

AUTHOR'S NOTES

The setting for this fictional story with its imaginary characters was adapted from an eighteenth century house in Portsmouth, New Hampshire — the 1716 MacPheadris Warner House — now a museum. There you will find a rooftop cupola, early murals of American Indians in all their colorful splendor and enjoy discovering a delightful mansion, long famous for its early Georgian architecture and its fine antique furnishings.

It is unlikely that an intact family such as Matty's ever lived in the slaves' quarters which used to be attached to the back of that building. However, in the MacPheadris Warner House between 1720 and the end of the eighteenth century, there are records of eight Africans — Quamino, Nero, Prince, Cato, Peter, John Jack, Phyllis, and an un-named girl — in addition to an "Indian boy" who were held as slaves for various, unknown periods of time. Almost nothing is known about them, their daily life, family structure, their masters' attitudes toward them or what finally happened to most of them. Two of the group, Peter and Cato, were among the twenty Africans who signed the failed freedom petition to the New Hampshire Assembly in 1779. (Unfortunately, New Hampshire never took straightforward steps to outlaw slavery. Instead, various rulings were issued merely to discourage it. Finally, in 1857, the State granted citizenship to all its Black residents.)

CHILD OUT OF PLACE was created as a way to introduce young people (and perhaps adults, also) to part of a different, mostly hidden chapter in the history of slavery in America — the New England chapter. Textbooks seldom, if ever, mention that chapter.

The stories told by the character, Bess, though in fictional form, do utilize some of what historical information exists regarding experiences and living conditions of enslaved Africans in a coastal New England town such as Portsmouth.

The best source of information regarding early Africans in Portsmouth, their developing community life, the African Court and their efforts to gain their freedom is THE PORTSMOUTH BLACK HERITAGE TRAIL by Valerie Cunningham and Mark Sammons (Portsmouth, NH, 1999) and also their forthcoming book entitled BLACK PORTSMOUTH to be published by University of New England Press in 2003. Resource material is also available at Portsmouth's Seacoast African American Cultural Center, the Portsmouth Athenaeum and Portsmouth Public Library. On the internet, visit www.seacoastnh.com/blackhistory/ and www.warnerhouse.org. For information on the African Meeting House in Boston, contact the Museum of Afro-American History at www.afroammuseum.org.

ACKNOWLEDGMENTS

A wise woman once told me that, in whatever we do, we are always guided by many minds — past as well as present. And so it was with the research and writing of this story. I am most grateful to the following people for their helpfulness and encouragement.

Valerie Cunningham, historian and author, has been my steadfast mentor, patiently guiding me toward understanding and authenticity in regard to the lives of early Africans in Portsmouth. Mark Sammons, co-author, with Ms. Cunningham of THE PORTSMOUTH BLACK HERITAGE TRAIL, kindly shared some of his extensive knowledge of Black history and American eighteenth century life and culture.

I am indebted to the Warner House Association and its Board of Governors for their support of this writing project. As a guide in the MacPheadris Warner House Museum for many years and as a former board member, I have a deep affection and concern for the House and for its continuing role in American history education.

To my friend and talented illustrator, Deborah Ronnquist, I express my joy and appreciation for her 'seeing' into my story to bring Matty and her world so skillfully and caringly into view.

Valerie Wall Hedrick, dear daughter, good friend, editor and wise counselor, helped me immeasurably throughout this project.

A heartfelt thank you also goes to those who took the time to read and comment on one or another draft of the manuscript: Lynn Aber, Caitlin Aber, Mr. and Mrs. Rhett Austell, Eve Barrett, Mr. and Mrs. Robert Barth, Maryellen Burke, Nancy Burns, Dr. Richard Candee, Elizabeth and Sidney

Acknowledgements

Carter, Deborah Child, Patricia Cirone, MacKenzie Covington, Merry Craig, William Cunningham, Ronan Donohue, Barbara Engelbach, Rose Eppard, Carleigh Erwin, Steve Fowle, Susan Hamilton, Thomas Hardiman, The Right Reverend Barbara C. Harris, Richard Haynes, Mr. and Mrs. Emerald C. Jackson, Marcia Jebb, Lawrence Kent, Holly Littlefield, Janet MacCracken, Corinne L. Mann, John O'Sullivan, Elizabeth Quigley Morgan, Jane Porter, Deborah Richards, Louise Richardson, Dennis Robinson, Susan Savory, Barbara Myers, Mr. and Mrs. Clinton Springer, Mr. and Mrs. Thaxter Swan, Judith Totman, Joyce Volk, and Mark Williams.

ABOUT THE AUTHOR: For Patricia Wall, the stray pieces of her life and career — journalism, radio, public relations and sales, house museum director, passion for the sea and American history, parent and grandparenthood, plus a move to Southern Maine at the doorstep of Portsmouth, NH — all came together somehow in the creation of this, her first book.

ABOUT THE ILLUSTRATOR: Debby Ronnquist's lively talent, a broad range of artistic media experience and a warm, caring nature are evident in all her work. Her creative skills also include sculpture, Russian iconography and clock dials. She is author of several needlework books and an expert in doll making. Debby and her family live in Southern Maine.

Give the gift of
CHILD OUT OF PLACE: A Story of New England
to your friends and family

Check Your Local Bookstore
or Order By Mail As Follows:

YES: I want _____ copies of CHILD OUT OF PLACE: A Story of
New England at $12.00 each ($18.00 Canadian)

Payment must be made either by check or money order.
Include $1.95 for shipping and handling for one book and $1.00
for each additional book. Maine residents must include applica-
ble sales tax. Canadian orders must include payments in US
funds.

Payment must accompany order.
Allow 3 weeks for delivery.

My ☐ check or ☐ money order for $_____ is enclosed.

Send to:

Name: _____

Address: _____

City: _____ State: _____ Zip: _____

Phone: _____

e-mail: _____
We respect your privacy and will not give out your address.

Make check or money order payable and return to:

FALL ROSE BOOKS
P.O. Box 39
Kittery Point, ME 03905

Web site: www.fallrosebooks.com